C000057856

Bello:
hidden talent rediscovered!

Bello is a digital only imprint of Pan Macmillan,
established to breathe new life into previously published,
classic books.

At Bello we believe in the timeless power of the imagination,
of good story, narrative and entertainment and we want to use
digital technology to ensure that many more readers
can enjoy these books into the future.

We publish in ebook and Print on Demand formats
to bring these wonderful books to new audiences.

About Bello:

www.panmacmillan.com/imprints/bello

About the author:

www.panmacmillan.com/author/francisdurbridge

By Francis Durbridge

Francis Durbridge

Francis Henry Durbridge was an English playwright and author born in Hull. In 1938, he created the character Paul Temple for the BBC radio serial *Send for Paul Temple*.

A crime novelist and detective, the gentlemanly Temple solved numerous crimes with the help of Steve Trent, a Fleet Street journalist who later became his wife. The character proved enormously popular and appeared in 16 radio serials and later spawned a 64-part big-budget television series (1969-71) and radio productions, as well as a number of comic strips, four feature films and various foreign radio productions.

Francis Durbridge also had a successful career as a writer for the stage and screen. His most successful play, *Suddenly at Home*, ran in London's West End for over a year.

Francis Durbridge

A GAME
OF MURDER

BELL◎

First published in 1975 by Hodder and Stoughton

This edition published 2012 by Bello
an imprint of Pan Macmillan, a division of Macmillan Publishers Limited
Pan Macmillan, 20 New Wharf Road, London N1 9RR
Basingstoke and Oxford
Associated companies throughout the world

www.panmacmillan.com/imprints/bello
www.curtisbrown.co.uk

ISBN 978-1-4472-1518-9 EPUB
ISBN 978-1-4472-1517-2 POD

Copyright © Francis Durbridge, 1975

The right of Francis Durbridge to be identified as the
author of this work has been asserted in accordance
with the Copyright, Designs and Patents Act 1988.

Every effort has been made to contact the copyright holders of the material
reproduced in this book. If any have been inadvertently overlooked, the publisher
will be pleased to make restitution at the earliest opportunity.

You may not copy, store, distribute, transmit, reproduce or otherwise
make available this publication (or any part of it) in any form, or by any means
(electronic, digital, optical, mechanical, photocopying, recording or otherwise),
without the prior written permission of the publisher. Any person who does
any unauthorized act in relation to this publication may be liable to
criminal prosecution and civil claims for damages.

The Macmillan Group has no responsibility for the information provided by
any author websites whose address you obtain from this book ('author websites').
The inclusion of author website addresses in this book does not constitute
an endorsement by or association with us of such sites or the content,
products, advertising or other materials presented on such sites.

A CIP catalogue record for this book is available from the British Library.

This book remains true to the original in every way. Some aspects may appear
out-of-date to modern-day readers. Bello makes no apology for this, as to retrospectively
change any content would be anachronistic and undermine the authenticity of the original.
Bello has no responsibility for the content of the material in this book. The opinions
expressed are those of the author and do not constitute an endorsement by,
or association with, us of the characterisation and content.

Visit **www.panmacmillan.com** to read more about all our books
and to buy them. You will also find features, author interviews and
news of any author events, and you can sign up for e-newsletters
so that you're always first to hear about our new releases.

Contents

Chapter 1

Douglas Croft parked his car in a side-street, checked the doors and boot to make sure he had locked them securely, then walked the fifty yards or so back to the Finchley Road. It was the morning rush-hour and traffic was streaming down from Swiss Cottage towards Lord's cricket ground about a quarter of a mile farther on.

Rather than move up the road to the pedestrian crossing, Douglas Croft chose his time and slipped across the road on a weaving course, rather like a centre forward cutting through the defences of an opposing team. He gained the footpath exactly opposite a shop window filled with sporting gear of every imaginable kind. Over the windows and entrance a sign proclaimed 'Tom Dawson's Sportstore'.

The neon light which burned all night to illuminate any possible intruder for the benefit of the patrolling police was still burning. As Douglas inserted the second of the two keys which were needed to open the shop door he glanced up and saw a girl coming across the crowded pavement. He opened the door and waited for her to go in past him.

'Morning, Liz. Did you see the guv'nor on Sports Profile last night?'

'No.' Liz shook her head and paused, glancing at the montage of blown-up photographs which occupied the centre of the window display. They were action-shots of Tom Dawson in his hey-day, when in the space of a single year he had represented England at rugby football and cricket and had also been runner-up in the Amateur Golf Championship. 'I didn't watch it last night.

It's my practice night and I have a race next weekend. One hundred metres back-stroke.'

She moved on into the shop. Douglas closed the door and turned one of the keys on the inside. There were still ten minutes till opening time. He collected the letters from the box and followed Liz Mason towards the small glass-partitioned office at the back of the shop. Not for the first time he took pleasure in watching the lithe way her trim figure moved. At nineteen Liz was like a breath of fresh ozone miraculously surviving in the fumes and dust of London.

'How did Mr. Dawson come over?' she asked over her shoulder. 'Nervous was he?'

Douglas gave a short laugh. 'Not him! What they call a strong screen image. He'll be getting his own show next.'

'Heaven forbid!' Liz exclaimed with feeling. She took her light showerproof coat off and hung it on the back of the office door.

Douglas slapped the wad of letters down on the desk and moved towards the switches which turned on the main shop lights and the spot lights used for display purposes in the front window. They brought into sharp relief glittering rows of matched golf irons, racks of tapering, varnished skis, a cabinet of extremely expensive pullovers, anoraks and waterproof garments, complex sets of equipment for skin divers, a bookcase containing volumes on every aspect of sport from tiddly-winks to big-game hunting.

'I had to laugh at one thing, though.' Subconsciously Douglas was smoothing his slightly wavy fair hair into better shape. The wind in the car had undone the careful attention he had given it before his mirror that morning. 'When the interviewer described his son as "the tough little glamour boy of Scotland Yard".'

'What nonsense ! Harry isn't tough – he's not as tough as his old man.'

Liz had let her voice rise. Douglas made a warning gesture with his finger, pointing towards the ceiling. A spiral staircase led out of the office to the flat above the shop, where Tom Dawson lived with his bachelor son.

'Do you think they could have heard?' Liz whispered.

'No. They keep the door of the box-room closed. But *I'll* be hearing from Mr. Tom Dawson if I don't get this mail sorted out before he comes down.'

If Douglas Croft could have seen through the ceiling of the shop into the flat above he would have realised that he had plenty of time in hand. Tom Dawson and his son were still sitting over breakfast in the dining area at one end of the large sitting-room.

When Tom Dawson had bought the place a few years earlier he had had the interior gutted and within the outer shell had created an ultra-modern ground-floor shop and on the floor above a comfortable, no-nonsense flat with accommodation for himself, his son and their resident cook-housekeeper.

The furniture in the living-room was of good quality and comfortable, but everything had its place and its purpose. There were no feminine frills, no vases of flowers, no displays of *objets d'art* cluttering the shelves. The glass-fronted cabinet containing the innumerable trophies won by Tom Dawson was more a challenge than a decoration.

There was little about Harry Dawson's appearance at that moment to justify the description used by the television commentator. He was wearing an open-necked shirt, faded blue slacks and a pair of bedroom slippers. The morning paper was propped against the tea-pot in front of him and he was just starting on his third cup.

Tom Dawson studied his son's profile and his pride showed on his face. The boy had inherited his own physical strength. He was tall and very well proportioned. But he also had a great deal of his mother's finesse. The dark good looks, that firm set to the mouth, those rather elusive and secretive blue eyes, so unusual with dark hair, had been inherited from her side. It had come as a surprise to Tom when Harry had announced his intention of making a career for himself in the Metropolitan Police, but he was already convinced that Harry would be a Commissioner before he was forty.

He broke the silence between them. 'I reckon you were about ready for this spot of leave, Harry.'

'Like it would have been next stop the psychiatrist's couch,

3

you mean?' Harry pushed his chair back and stretched his legs luxuriously. 'I must say it's great to think I don't have to go near the Yard or listen to old man Yardley for two whole weeks.'

Tom Dawson noted an edge of bitterness in his son's voice. 'I have the impression you haven't been getting on too well with the Superintendent just lately, Harry.'

'*Chief*-Superintendent, if you don't mind. That's very important to him now. Oh, I've been getting on with him all right. It's just that he doesn't get on with me. Still, Yardley's not a bad chap, I suppose – just an over-worked and irritable old cuss.'

Tom Dawson nodded sympathetically. He stood up and moved across to the spacious mahogany antique desk placed between the two windows of the room. On it stood two telephones, one Post Office instrument and another private set for intercommunication with the shop below, along with other items of office equipment which showed that he was in the habit of doing the greater part of his business up here in the flat. No one who saw the lightness of his step would have guessed that Tom Dawson was already in his early sixties. He had weathered the years well because he had 'taken pains to keep himself fit, to prevent the muscle on his powerful frame from turning to fat.

'By the way, Dad.' Harry finished off his last cup and folded the newspaper. 'I've changed my mind about going away. I'd rather just stay here, take things quietly and potter about for a couple of weeks – if that's okay by you.'

'Sure,' Tom said, trying not to show how much pleasure his son's casual announcement had given him. Even after twelve years of widowhood he could still at times feel agonisingly lonely. 'Whatever you like, Harry.'

He reached across the desk, picked up the intercom phone and pressed the buzzer. After a few seconds Douglas Croft's voice came through from the office below. It had acquired a nasal, metallic quality during its trip through fifty feet of cable.

'Good morning, Mr. Dawson.'

'Morning, Douglas.' Tom Dawson did not have to raise his strong, deep voice to give it carrying power. 'I shall probably be out all day. If Harris Brothers phone, just stall. I'll talk to them tomorrow.'

'Yes. All right.'

Down in the office Douglas was rapidly flipping through the letters he had opened, trying to decide if there was anything which urgently needed his employer's attention.

'There's a—'

'Yes?'

'There's a reply from Allied Sports. It's not very satisfactory, I'm afraid.'

'What do they say?' Tom Dawson could hear the rustle of papers and Douglas clearing his throat. No. Don't read it out to me. Bring it up. And Douglas – Bring me some golf balls. Better make it half a dozen of the Dunlop 65s.'

He put the receiver back on its cradle and returned to the breakfast table. He did not look directly at his son but he could feel those blue eyes studying his face.

'Who are you playing today, Dad?'

'What? Oh – ah – no one in particular. My game's been a bit off lately. I thought I'd just play a few practice holes on my own.'

'But that's great!' Harry exclaimed enthusiastically. 'I haven't got anything fixed up for today.'

'Hm?'

'I'll give you a game.'

Tom Dawson's brows furrowed slightly and it seemed to Harry that his sun-tanned cheeks coloured slightly.

'Well, thanks, Harry – but actually—'

'I thought so.' Harry cut into his father's hesitant excuses. 'Thought what?'

'Come on. Who's the mystery opponent? Who is it?'

Reluctantly Tom Dawson met his son's eyes. 'You damned CID men!'

'Some mini-skirted dolly bird you've got hold of, I expect.' Harry bit off his laugh when he saw the suddenly serious expression on the older man's face.

'Credit me with more taste than that, lad,' he said quietly.

Knowing that his father was going to say more Harry remained silent. He waited expectantly. After a few moments Tom Dawson grinned wryly and shrugged his shoulders.

'Yes, well, I suppose it is about time you met. About time. Look, Harry, why don't you come up to the club-house about midday? We should be through by then. We can all have a drink together. How about that?'

Tom Dawson's expression and his sudden enthusiasm made him look ten years younger.

'I can't wait,' Harry said sincerely. 'Had I better change into – '

His question was cut off when the door leading from the sitting-room into the kitchen abruptly opened and Mrs. Rogers thrust her way into the room, wiping her hands on the apron she was wearing.

The Dawsons' housekeeper had shown herself, soon after her employment, to be something of a battle-axe who believed that her mission in life was to keep these two unattached males in order. Now, however, all the old fire had gone out of her. There were worry lines round her eyes and mouth and her whole body seemed to sag with depression.

'Would you like some more toast, Mr. Harry?'

'No, thank you, Mrs. Rogers.' Harry pushed his chair back and stood up. 'We've really finished, if you want to clear away.'

Mrs. Rogers nodded and moved towards the table. Quite obviously her query had been meant to indicate that breakfast should have been finished long ago.

'There's no news of that dog of yours, I suppose?' Tom Dawson enquired.

Harry turned away and raised his eyes despairingly towards heaven, but Mrs. Rogers seized eagerly on the question. She came round the edge of the table, forgetting all about clearing up the dirty dishes.

'No, I'm afraid not, Mr. Dawson. I rang up the R.S.P.C.A. last night to see if they could help, but of course they couldn't.' She shook her head mournfully. 'It's always the same. No one seems to bother – no one wants to know.'

Irritated by the woman's tone of self-pity, Harry turned round. 'Well, we're bothering, Mrs. Rogers; we're doing everything we can.'

He strode across to the breakfast table, picked up the newspaper and thrust the open page before her. 'The advertisement is in the local paper and they've even published the photograph I sent them.'

Mrs. Rogers' eyes moistened with tenderness and grief as she gazed at the photograph. It portrayed an extremely pampered and cock-sure poodle, sitting on its hind legs and begging for a biscuit. Round its neck it wore an ornate collar, more suited to the wrist of some pop star. Under the picture was the caption : 'HAVE YOU SEEN ZERO?'

'Yes. I know you're all doing all you can, Mr. Harry. I wasn't referring to you.' She put up a finger to wipe a tear from the corner of her eye. But it's nearly a week now since Zero disappeared. And he was wearing his collar, that's what I don't understand.'

The housekeeper reached for her handkerchief and blew her nose. She turned her eyes towards Tom Dawson. 'He was wearing that lovely little collar you gave him for his birthday.'

Tom Dawson cleared his throat and glanced at Harry, as if for inspiration.

'Yes, well – ah. Never mind, Mrs. Rogers. Now come on, pull yourself together. It's not the end of the world, you know.'

'Yes,' Harry joined in. 'Cheer up, Mrs. Rogers. No news is good news.'

'I think I'd like some more, tea, Mrs. Rogers,' Tom Dawson said suddenly. 'Would you please make another pot?'

Mrs. Rogers straightened a little, like a flagging soldier called to attention by the sergeant-major. She made an obvious effort to pull herself together, gave a quick nod and retreated to the kitchen, taking the tea-pot with her.

'That bloody poodle!' Dawson exclaimed as soon as the door had shut.

'She's making a meal of it, I'm afraid.'

'The trouble is, lad, she thinks that you ought to be able to find him – just like that.'

Tom Dawson snapped his fingers. Harry contemplated the closed kitchen door, smiling.

'Yes, I know. In her eyes I must be the worst detective in the whole of England.'

The sound of steps on the spiral staircase that led up into the adjoining room had a way of reverberating through the steel girders which supported the rebuilt flat. So it was no surprise when the door of the box-room opened and Douglas Croft poked his fair head through.

'May I come in?'

'Yes, of course. Come along in, Douglas.'

Douglas gave Harry the benefit of his frank and disarming smile. 'Good morning, Harry.'

'Morning, old boy.' Harry nodded, picked up the newspaper and settled himself in one of the leather arm-chairs facing the fireplace.

'Douglas placed the box of golf balls which he was carrying on the end of the desk and handed Tom Dawson a sheet of typed notepaper which he had brought up in a folder.

'You came across very well on television last night, Mr. Dawson.'

'You think so?' Dawson was obviously pleased at this comment.

Douglas nodded emphatically. 'Should pull in a few extra customers if I know anything about it.'

From the kitchen came the sound of a shattering crash followed by an exclamation of dismay. Tom Dawson said good-bye to his second cup of tea and made a mental note to add 'new teapot' to the shopping list. Douglas, after a startled glance at the kitchen door, extracted another letter from his folder.

'As you say, the Allied Sports reply is not very satisfactory.' Tom Dawson exchanged the first letter for the one Douglas was now proffering him.

'This is a reply from Houston. He wants to drop in and see you—'

'There's no point in his seeing me.' Dawson spoke with sudden venom. 'The rackets were faulty. They've got to take them back.'

Douglas consulted the notes he had jotted on the inside flap of the folder. He decided he had better stick to essentials. The old man seemed terribly impatient this morning, not so much because these replies angered him as because he was anxious to despatch the business and be on his way.

'You've made a note for me to phone Swim-Dive. I don't know what about, Mr. Dawson.'

Dawson was still immersed in the letter from the racket suppliers.

'What? Oh, yes. Don't worry about that, Douglas. I've seen to it.'

Douglas closed the folder and stared at some figures written on the outside cover.

'And you've jotted down what looks like—' He was holding the folder at an angle to read the figures. 'A car number, for some reason or other.'

Dawson looked up sharply.

'A car number?'

'Yes. Here on the cover. It's JKY 384 L.'

'I don't know what on earth that is,' Dawson said impatiently. 'Ask Liz about it. She probably wrote it down. You know, this letter is a damned impertinence! It's just begging the issue.'

Dawson was still scowling over the offending document when the kitchen door opened and Mrs. Rogers came through, clearly in a very contrite mood.

'Good Morning, Mrs. Rogers,' Douglas Croft greeted her enthusiastically with his flashing smile.

'Oh!' Mrs. Rogers seemed embarrassed to find three men facing her. 'Good morning, Mr. Croft.'

'Any news of Zero?' Douglas continued brightly. He realised at once that he had put his foot in it. Tom Dawson flashed him a look of utter exasperation.

Mrs. Rogers turned towards Douglas Croft as a homing pigeon heads for its loft.

'No. I'm afraid not, Mr. Croft. I've tried the R.S.P.C.A. to see if they can help but it seems that they just don't want to know.

And though they've put Zero's photograph in the paper nobody has come forward. I just can't understand it, because he was wearing that lovely little collar—'

The housekeeper was in full spate again. Tom Dawson left Douglas to cope with what he had started and drifted over to where his son was seated. Harry looked up over his paper and the two men exchanged a glance of mutual understanding.

'Here we go again,' Harry mouthed.

With nothing special to do Harry had been enjoying the luxury of simply killing time. He had set off for the golf club earlier than he needed, so that he could take things easy on the drive. Approaching Westgate Golf Club he was simply dawdling. It was not yet twelve o'clock and he did not want to arrive before the midday rendezvous his father had given him. He sensed that his meeting was going to be an important one, might even mark a turning point in Tom Dawson's life. It could turn out to be only another business deal; Tom Dawson liked to clinch 'his agreements in the club-house after a game of golf. But somehow Harry felt that this was different, especially when he remembered his father's serious expression when he had said : 'Credit me with more taste than that, lad.' If it was a woman Harry hoped that his father had not fallen for some young girl. Tom Dawson would look foolish married to one of those dolly-birds he had so flippantly referred to at breakfast.

The all too familiar noise of a siren sounded behind him, breaking into his reverie. Glancing in his mirror he could see the blue light flashing on the roof of an ambulance coming up fast behind him. He pulled over, lowered his window and signalled it on by hand. It tore past, the shock-wave of air rocking his own car.

Following at a more sober pace Harry saw the ambulance brake, cut boldly across the bows of an on-coming truck and turn in to the entrance to Westgate Golf Club. At the same point he himself had to wait for some considerable time to allow an oncoming stream of cars to pass. When at last he made the turn he found himself accelerating hard up the tree-lined private road that led to the club. And he could not have said whether it was the son or the policeman in him which gave him that sudden sense of urgency.

When he came in sight of the club-house the ambulance had drawn up outside the doorway. One of the uniformed attendants had dismounted and was talking to the club secretary. Commander Whitby was pointing out across the golf course. Harry saw his arm sweep round as he indicated a grassy track, Used by service vehicles, which wound its way towards the sixth green and the eighth tee.

As the attendant jumped aboard and the ambulance moved away, the secretary ran for his own estate car. Before he reached it Harry's Austin 1100 had braked to a halt beside him. The secretary looked round and when he saw who the driver was his strained expression changed.

'Mr. Dawson. Thank heavens you've come.'

Harry had the door open and one leg out. 'What's going on?'

'It's your father.' The secretary's eyes shifted away from Harry's intent gaze. 'He's – there's been an accident.'

'What do you mean?'

'So far as we can make out he was practising down by the sixth green – your father that is – and – well, you know how the ground falls away steeply to the brook—'

'*What* accident?' Harry cut in icily.

'A drive. A drive hooked off the eighth tee. It seems it struck your father full pitch on the back of the head and – Luckily Dr. Roach was in the club-house. He went straight out and—'

'How bad?' Harry said, forcing himself to keep his voice level. 'How bad is it?'

'Well, Dr. Roach was with him when I came back to phone for the ambulance but I'm afraid – his head hit a stone in the brook.'

'Jump in,' Harry said suddenly. 'I'm going to follow that ambulance.'

The secretary scrambled into the passenger seat. Harry set off along the grass track, not caring if his suspension took a hammering from the uneven ground. The ambulance had already disappeared, swaying ominously, into the hilly section of the course – referred to feelingly by the members as The Himalayas. Neither he nor the secretary spoke another word till they came over the top of a rise and found the sixth green in a little hollow below them.

The sixth hole was a very tricky Par 3. The green was hidden from the tee so the drive of some 190 yards was a blind one. And the length had to be just right, for a set of bunkers were waiting to trap a ball which fell short and a drive hit too strongly would finish up in the deep burn just beyond the green.

It was from this steep-sided burn that the two ambulance men were lifting a body. They laid it on the mown grass edging the green and moved to fetch the stretcher from the ambulance.

Dr. Roach was squatting at the top of the bank, packing his instruments into the suitcase which every doctor keeps in the back of his car. He glanced up as Harry slammed the door of the Austin and walked quickly over. Harry had played the doctor in the early rounds of a club tournament, and he could not help liking the small, greying and slightly fussy G.P.

'How bad is he, Doctor Roach?'

Dr. Roach straightened up with something of an effort and looked compassionately at Harry.

'I'm deeply sorry, Mr. Dawson, but your father's dead. He must have been killed by the fall.'

Harry had been in the presence of sudden, violent death before and had learned not to be unduly affected by it. But when he looked down at the still form with its blood-soaked head and twisted grimace he had to make a violent effort to control himself.

'Killed?' he repeated incredulously.

'It was probably instantaneous. The blow from the golf ball stunned him and he fell down this steep bank into the stream. There's so little water in it now that the stones are all exposed. He cracked his head on one of the large boulders. I don't suppose he knew a thing about what happened—'

Harry stood back to let the ambulance men place his father

on the pull-out stretcher they had brought from the ambulance. His gaze never left the scarred face till the attendant pulled up the blanket, hiding it for ever from his sight.

Only then did Detective Inspector Harry Dawson lift his eyes to record the scene around him.

The sun had broken through the morning clouds and the course was looking particularly beautiful. Yellow flowers speckled the dreaded gorse bushes to the left of the green. His father's golf-bag lay on the grass at the edge of the green. Three or four of the new Dunlop 65s had spilled from the pocket. Standing in a ring but keeping at a respectful distance were a couple of groundsmen and half a dozen players who had been drawn to the spot by the unusual sight of an ambulance swaying across the eighth fairway. A little apart, talking to the secretary in whispers, was a young man of about thirty. He had a small selection of clubs in a light bag over his shoulder and was emphatically dressed for golf, so much so that he might have posed as a model for some fashionable brand of sportswear. And he had the rather exaggerated good looks to carry it off.

At the moment, however, he was nervous and distressed. He moved tentatively towards Harry and spoke in a quiet, low voice.

'Mr. Dawson, I want you to know how – dear God, I wouldn't have had this happen for—'

His voice tailed off. Harry did not stop watching the blanketed form being carefully loaded into the ambulance.

'Who are you?'

'I'm Peter Newton. I was out practising. I drove a ball off the eighth tee up there and sliced it badly—'

'The eighth tee?'

'Yes. I've been trying to cure this slice—'

Once again Harry cut through the man's hesitant excuses. He spun round towards the secretary.

'Have you notified the police?'

'The police?' the secretary echoed and his mouth remained open.

'Naturally,' Harry said, and then, as he saw the Commander

hesitating, he suddenly exploded. 'Damn it, a man has been killed here!'

'Of course.' Commander Whitby nodded and finally got his mouth closed. He turned away and hurried off in the direction of the club-house.

Harry now for the first time directed the cold stare of his blue eyes at Peter Newton.

'Where's his friend?'

'I'm sorry?'

'The person he was playing with. Where is he?'

The clubs rattled in Peter Newton's bag as he turned to look round him helplessly.

'As far as I know he – your father was alone.'

'You're sure of that?'

'Well, I certainly did not see anyone. The moment I saw I'd sliced my drive towards him I yelled out "fore". But he can't have heard me. When I saw I'd hit him, you can imagine. I dashed across. He'd fallen down the bank, was lying down there, right in the bed of the stream. His head was—'

'And no one with him?'

Peter Newton shook his head. 'No one when I got here. Mr. Dawson, this is the most terrible thing that's ever happened to me. I mean, as I was just trying to explain—'

Harry turned away from the pleading face. 'Save it, Mr. Newton. Save your explanations for the police officer in charge of the investigation.'

Ten yards away the ambulance doors were slammed shut, providing an emphatic punctuation mark to Harry's terse statement.

'An accident,' Harry said. 'He kept calling it an accident. Damn fool of a Divisional Inspector. How can he know at this stage? I tried, Nat, I tried to tell him. But—'

'But he told you to mind your own business.'

'More or less, yes. As you know I'm on annual leave just now – *persona non grata* and all that. Would you be a mate and get on to him for me?'

'Yes, of course.' Nat's voice faded in the telephone receiver as he turned away, probably reaching for a memo pad. 'What's his name?'

'Carter. And if he's still saying there's no suspicion of foul play. I suggest you—'

'Leave it with me, Harry,' Nat cut in reassuringly. Harry realised that his personal involvement in this thing was impelling him to talk rather emotionally. 'Leave it with me. I'll be back to you as soon as I can.'

'Thanks, Nat.'

Harry replaced the receiver and leaned back with a sigh of relief. He was seated at his father's desk, which was still littered with eloquent reminders of the man who had been using it only a few hours before and now lay in the police mortuary. Nat Fletcher was a colleague of Harry's and a good friend. It was better to leave him to tackle the officious and self-important Carter.

Douglas Croft had come up the spiral staircase and entered the room just as the telephone conversation had begun. Harry had signalled him to stay and listen to what he was saying. Now he turned to Douglas, who was hovering just inside the door, an expression of bewilderment on his sun-tanned face.

'Harry, do you – do you think there's suspicion of foul play?'

Harry did not answer for a moment. He was studying his father's engagement diary, which lay open on the desk. 'Suspicion? Yes. Yes, I do, Douglas.'

He stood up and crossed the room to a corner cabinet where the drinks and glasses were kept. He found the whisky bottle, poured a measure and added the same amount from the bottle of Malvern water.

'A man dies of severe head injuries,' he said over his shoulder. 'He was supposed to be playing golf with some person unknown. That person has not yet been traced. Blood was found on a large stone beside the brook.'

Harry made a gesture towards the drinks cupboard and Douglas shook his head, refusing the unspoken invitation. He was too intent on Harry's words to be diverted by anything else.

Harry walked into the middle of the room, staring into the glass of whisky as if it were a crystal-gazer's bowl.

'And a man comes forward, Douglas – A man comes forward claiming to have sliced a practice-drive from a tee two hundred and twenty yards away.'

'A pretty long way to hit a slice,' Douglas murmured.

'A drive,' Harry continued slowly, 'which stunned my father, causing him to fall into the stream—'

'Your father?'

Both men turned in surprise. Mrs. Rogers, dressed for the street and still holding the basket of goods she had bought in the supermarket, was standing in the doorway leading through from the kitchen.

Her face had gone very pale. She seemed to have sensed that something terrible was about to be revealed to her. 'Has something happened to Mr. Dawson?'

'Come and sit down, Mrs. Rogers.' Harry hurried across to relieve her of the basket before she dropped it on the floor. 'Over here on this chair. I'm afraid it's all very sudden and tragic.'

'He – Is he – ?' Mrs. Rogers surrendered the basket but made no move towards the chair.

'My father died this morning, Mrs. Rogers. He was killed out on the golf course.'

'K-killed?' The word half stuck in the housekeeper's throat.

Douglas Croft interposed, hoping to lessen the shock. 'It could have been an accident, Mrs. Rogers.'

Harry turned on him angrily. 'He was deliberately killed!'

The eyes of Douglas, directed over his shoulder, widened in alarm. Harry spun round and saw Mrs. Rogers sway. He reached her just in time to take her weight before she crumpled to the floor.

'Quick, Douglas, get those things off the settee.'

While Harry supported the very considerable weight of Mrs. Rogers' inert and sagging form, Douglas gathered up the books and magazines that littered the settee. Harry dragged her over and placed her on the cushions so that her legs were above the level of her head.

'Shall I fetch some water?' Douglas suggested.

'Hm?' Harry was staring in surprise at the limp face with its closed eyes. 'Oh, yes.' Then he added, more to himself: 'I'd hardly have thought she—'

By the time Douglas returned from the kitchen with the glass of water Mrs. Rogers' eyelids had begun to flutter. Harry supported her head so that she could drink.

'Here, Mrs. Rogers. Have a sip of this and then we'll get the kettle on for a cup of tea.'

Mrs. Rogers ignored the words and the glass of water. Her eyes were wide open now, staring past Harry, past the wall of the room. She was in a state of shock.

She ran her tongue over her lips and whispered just one word. 'Dead.'

Harry despairingly surveyed the chaos on the breakfast table and the utter confusion which he had succeeded in creating in the kitchen. His watch told him that it was half-past nine. He would not have believed that it could take him so long to prepare and eat his breakfast, even with the whisky which he had polished off the night before befuddling his brain.

When the private door-bell rang he wondered whether to ignore it. He was still in his pyjamas and dressing-gown and had not shaved. It was in any case probably another of those infernal reporters. But the ring of the bell was followed by a sharp ratatat on the knocker which somehow gave an impression of authority. Pushing his fingers through his hair Harry went out into the hall and down the flight of stairs to the private entrance at the side of the shop.

On the threshold stood a rugged man in his early forties. His hair was neatly clipped, his eyes alert and restless. He wore a short blue raincoat and his hands hung at his sides as if ready to make some sudden movement of defence or attack.

'Nat!' Harry exclaimed with pleasure. 'Come on in.'

Nat nodded amicably and began to follow Harry up the stairs.

'How are you feeling this morning, old chap?'

'Somewhat numbed still, thoroughly hung over, pestered half out of my mind by the ruddy newspaper reporters.'

Harry stood back to let his guest enter the sitting-room first. 'Come on through.'

'Look.' Nat Fletcher's voice was gruff. 'I know I said this yesterday on the phone, but I really am most deeply sorry about your father.'

'Yes. Sure. Thanks, Nat.' Harry waved his hand helplessly at the mess on the breakfast table and the general disorder in the room. Nat's sharp eyes had already summed up the situation and he had not missed the envelope propped prominently on the mantelpiece.

'Sorry about the mess. Mrs. Rogers, the housekeeper – she suddenly upped and left me. Left a note of apology saying her beloved nephew Hubert has 'flu, of all things.'

'Considerate of her – under the circumstances.'

'Frankly, what with the fuss she made about my father's death, I'm not all that sorry to have her out of the place. Went all to pieces over it, she did. It was bad enough when she lost her dog. But this—'

Nat cleared his throat. 'Sometimes, Harry, it can be the best thing to give vent to your feelings.'

It was the older man speaking to the younger. 'Sure,' Harry's voice showed a hint of resentment. 'And maybe some of us have different ways of showing it. So what news from that nit-wit Inspector Carter? He still talking about accidents?'

Nat had unbuttoned his raincoat but did not take it off. He surveyed Harry's face appraisingly, noting the signs of stress and fatigue. Although these two were good friends that did not prevent them from often disagreeing.

'Now, Harry, if you're going to be difficult over this—'

'Difficult!' Harry exploded. 'He was my father, and you expect me to sit back and—'

'And leave it to the professionals, right.'

'You have *seen* Carter?'

'Of course I've seen him. And he's neither a nit-wit nor is he the type to miss out on things.'

'What's he make of Newton's story? Does he believe it?'

'Look.' Nat spoke briskly, as if to an unreasonable child. 'Newton had never met your father. They were complete strangers to each other. The man was out practising. He sliced an unlucky drive. Damn it, the best golfer in the world couldn't be sure of hitting a man over two hundred yards away.'

'*If* it did happen that way.'

Nat frowned but Harry continued doggedly. 'Did they find the ball yet? Forensics would be able to tell if it really hit him as Newton says. And what about the stone he's supposed to have fallen on?'

'What about it?'

'Have you seen the post-mortem report yet? Surely the pathologist can tell—'

'Of course he can. And when he and the lab, boys have all finished their tests, that'll be the time to start questioning the validity of Newton's-statement. Then and not before.'

'All right, all right.' Harry yanked on the ends of his dressing-gown belt, knotting it more tightly. 'So what about this person my father was going to play with? The person he said he was going to introduce me to at the club-house afterwards. What about him?'

Nat was already buttoning his raincoat up again. 'Carter's making enquiries, of course. But so far, Harry, no one's been found to corroborate that theory.'

'Theory?'

'In fact,' Nat continued in his quiet, emphatic voice, 'the club professional says he's pretty certain he saw your father going out on to the course alone.'

Before Harry could find a suitable comment to this statement, the telephone started to ring.

'If that's another newspaper—'

Nat was already moving towards the door, grateful for the excuse to break off this gritty conversation.

'Look. I've got to get on. I'll let you know the moment there's any developments. Okay?'

'Okay,' Harry agreed morosely.

He waited till the door had closed on Nat, kicking himself inwardly for being so brittle. He could not afford to antagonise a good friend like Nat.

The caller was persistent. Harry resigned himself to answering the steady summons of the telephone.

A few miles away in a luxurious residence within a stone's throw of Hampstead Heath a woman was listening to the ringing tone in the earpiece of her mock-antique telephone. She was determined to ring for two full minutes before giving up.

She was, statistically speaking, in her early fifties, but she had preserved her excellent figure by declining to have children and her facial features by frequent treatments at beauty parlours.

Her surroundings provided a suitable setting. The drawing-room offered a marked contrast with the Dawson sitting-room. It was at the same time opulent and comfortable. Each item showed the influence of a woman with enough money to indulge her expensive taste.

While she waited she gazed at her reflection in the mirror behind the telephone. Sybil Conway liked to watch herself while she conversed with the unseen person at the other end of the line.

'Hallo.'

She glanced down at the pad on the telephone table. 'Is that 586 2679?'

'Yes.'

'My name is Conway. Mrs. Conway. There's an advertisement in our local paper about a poodle—'

'Yes. That's right.'

'Is the dog yours, Mr. – ah?'

'Dawson. No, it's my housekeeper's, but I am responsible for the advertisement. Have you found the poodle, Mrs. Conway?'

'Yes.' She gave a little laugh. 'At least I think so.'

She liked the sound of his voice: It had a kind of masculine harshness about it. She smiled at herself in the mirror. She knew from experience that this device made her own voice more alluring.

'It looks like the one in the paper – only a little dishevelled, I'm afraid. Actually my husband found it last night in the garden.'

'Where are you speaking from, Mrs. Conway?'

'We're in Hampstead. The house is called "Stillwater". It's in Broadway Avenue. Do you kno* Hampstead at all, Mr. Dawson?'

'Yes, I do.'

'It's a large house, just on the corner. It stands back from the road. The drive's on the right-hand side.'

'Will you be in this morning?'

'Yes. We are here all day. You can drop in any time.' 'Thank you, Mrs. Conway. It's very kind of you to have phoned.'

He replaced the receiver before she did. She hung the instrument up thoughtfully, then let her eyes drop to the open newspaper on the table. It showed the photo of Zero, begging for his biscuit, with his pretty collar round his neck.

'All right, Zero. You've kissed me three times now. That's enough.'

Harry was restraining the little black poodle on his knee. Zero had still not got over his joy at seeing an old friend and kept making sudden pecks with a very wet nose at Harry's face. It was hard to control the wriggling bundle of life. The collar which had been round his neck when he'd gone missing was no longer there.

Mrs. Conway was seated at the other end of the damask-covered settee, her well-shaped legs crossed gracefully. Arnold Conway, though seated, had the advantage of mobility. He was ensconced in a very new and modern wheelchair, which he seemed to enjoy swinging round into different positions. Perhaps to compensate for being a cripple he was meticulously dressed. Harry estimated that he was a little younger than his wife.

'Naturally,' he was saying, 'I was very surprised when I saw the animal. He was behind one of the rhododendron bushes, perfectly docile, almost asleep. I thought – well, blow me, how the devil did you get here?'

Hands on the polished chromium rings which enabled him to control the wheels, he swung his chair round and propelled himself towards the french windows which opened out on to a lawn bordered by shrubs.

'He's been missing over a week now. We'd given up hope of

ever seeing him again.' Harry held Zero's head still and made him meet his eyes. 'Where have you been, Zero? What the devil happened to you?'

Mrs. Conway intervened. 'You say he was wearing a collar when he disappeared?'

'Yes, a very nice one. My father gave it to Mrs. Rogers for her birthday.'

'For *her* birthday, not the poodle's!'

Mrs. Conway's laughter was infectious. Harry found himself laughing also.

Conway had swung his chair round again and moved it down to the settee.

'Some long-haired character picked him up in his car, I expect; then pinched the collar and booted him out.'

He put out a hand to pet Zero, but the dog growled warn ingly. Conway laughed the snub off.

'You've had a rough time, old chap, but I expect that mistress of yours will make it up to you.'

'That's then understatement of the year,' Harry said with feeling. Holding the poodle against his chest he rose from the settee. 'Mr. Conway, there was a, reward mentioned in the advertisement, five pounds, I think it was—'

'Mr. Dawson, please—' Mrs. Conway raised a delicate hand in horror at the mention of money.

'Don't be silly, old man.' Conway reversed a few yards back. 'We're only too happy to have found the little chap.'

He was heading towards the door as if to usher Harry out, when a sudden thought struck him. He wheeled round, smiling with mischievous pleasure at his idea.

'I suppose you wouldn't like to give the fiver to charity?'

'Darling!' protested Sybil Conway mildly.

'Now, don't be squeamish, old girl. Why do you think they gave me the job? I'm President of the "Hamsters", Mr. Dawson. Perhaps you've heard of us?'

'Er – no. I'm afraid I haven't.'

'We're a local society. What the Yanks would call "a bunch of do-gooders". We help the old age pensioners, look after the poor kids of the district, put on the odd show when we feel like it – in aid of charity, of course. Last year we collected well over eight hundred pounds.'

Harry put Zero down on the floor. The poodle immediately jumped up on to the cushions beside Mrs. Conway.

'Why, of course. I shall be delighted to give you a donation.'

'Thank you, Mr. Dawson.'

'Arnold, you really are a monster!'

'Nonsense, Sybil. Every bob counts these days, you know that.' Conway winked at Harry. 'Make the cheque out to Basil Higgs, old man. He's our secretary. H-I-G-G-S.'

Mrs. Conway was caressing the ears of Zero, who had snuggled against her thigh. She gestured towards a Sheraton writing table.

'You can use the desk over there, Mr. Dawson.'

Pulling his cheque book from his pocket, Harry crossed to the table, sat down and felt for his pen.

'I expect you'll hear from Basil,' Conway said, making a short tour round the back of the settee. 'He's bound to drop you a line.'

Mrs. Conway laughed again. 'You'll hear from him, all right. twice a year.'

Harry smiled, opened his cheque book and began to write the name of Basil Higgs.

Liz was alone in the shop and dealing with a customer when she saw Harry come clattering down the spiral staircase that led from the flat above. He was still wearing the overcoat he had gone out in and seemed to be in a great hurry. She dealt with the customer as quickly as she could and then went to the office at the back of the shop. Harry was seated at the desk, pulling open drawers and searching through their contents. His manner was very tense and urgent.

'Can I help, Mr. Dawson?'

Harry did not look up. He found a stack of folders in a bottom drawer and was checking through them. 'Where's that folder, Liz?'

'What folder do you mean, Mr.Dawson?'

'Douglas brought it up ,yesterday morning. It's just an ordinary blue folder, but there was a number scribbled on it – a car registration number.'

'A car number?'

'Yes. JKY 384. At least I think that was it. I want to make certain.'

Liz shook her head, trying to remember where she had seen a blue folder.

The spiral staircase, which continued on down into the basement, was again resounding to the sound of footsteps. The head of Douglas Croft came into view. He was carrying a stack of boxes which he had collected from the store.

Harry turned towards him. 'Douglas. Do you remember that folder which you brought up yesterday with the letters in it? A blue folder?'

'Yes.'

'Where is it?'

Douglas hesitated, struck by the urgency in Harry's voice. Without a word he handed the stack of boxes to Liz, who took them and went out into the shop. Douglas crossed to a letter tray and lifted it to reveal the blue folder. He handed it to Harry.

Harry turned it sideways to look at the cover. 'I knew damn well I was right.'

He pointed at the letters and figures jotted on the cardboard. 'This number, Douglas, JKY 384 L. You asked my father about it.'

'Yes. I didn't know what it was. I thought he'd made a note of it for some reason or other. He said he hadn't, but I'm sure it's his handwriting.'

'I saw the number this morning,' Harry said quietly. It was on a Fiat estate car. I got held up at traffic lights on the Finchley road. This car rushed up beside me on the inside, so close that it almost scraped me. There was a man and a girl in it and they were having the father and mother of a row. The girl was about twenty and rather good-looking. I didn't see the man's face till he turned to watch the traffic lights. Then I recognised him as Peter Newton.'

'That's the chap who drove the golf ball which—'

'Right.'

Douglas took the folder from Harry's hand and studied the figures on it.

'Are you sure of this, Harry?'

'Absolutely sure. When the lights changed he let his clutch in with a bang and shot ahead. I was able to see the registration number quite clearly. It was definitely JKY 384 L.'

Harry stood up and went to the rack which held the London telephone directories. He picked out the volume L-R, laid it on the desk and found the Ns. He ran his finger through half the Newtons listed till he found the initial P.

Leaning with one elbow on a tall filing cabinet Douglas watched while Harry dialled the number. It was answered almost at once, as if the call was expected.

'589-1872.'

'Peter Newton?'

A short pause, then, hesitantly: 'Yes. Who is it?'

'This is Harry Dawson.'

'Oh, Mr. Dawson. I've been wondering whether to phone you myself.'

'You have?'

'Yes. To say how dreadfully sorry I am for the tragic—'

Harry interrupted briskly : 'I'd like to see you, Newton. When can we meet?'

'Well, I – I'm workng till seven and then I have a dinner date.'

'What time will you be back?'

'About half-past ten, I suppose.'

'I'll see you then,' Harry said firmly. He consulted the entry in the telephone book. '3 Linton Close, Chelsea?'

'Yes. It's rather difficult to find, Mr. Dawson. It's in a mews near Sloane Square.'

'Don't worry. I'll find it.'

'Come straight up. I'm on the first floor.'

'Right. Half-past ten.'

Harry slammed the phone down and looked up at Douglas Croft. The fair-haired young man was watching him thoughtfully.

Harry had located the exact whereabouts of Linton Close by looking it up in the police guide to London streets. The car radio gave him a time check at 10.30 just as the dark green Austin 1100 was turning out of Sloane Square into the cul-de-sac which now bore the flattering name of Linton Close. It had at one time been a mews where the gentry of nearby Belgravia stabled their horses and carriages, with quarters overhead for the grooms and ostlers. An imaginative property developer had transformed it into a passable resemblance of an intimate village street, the only difference being the predominance of garage doors at street level.

The mews was dimly lit by several antique coach lamps outside doorways. He spotted a Fiat estate car parked near the far end of the mews and stopped his own car about twenty yards short of it. He removed the ignition key but did not lock the car. Some resident might want to push it back or forward to gain access to a garage.

From one of the lighted but curtained windows came the sound of somebody's hi-fi equipment playing Berlioz. Harry noted the lavish window-boxes and gaily painted doors, his sight gradually attuning itself to the dim lighting. His eyes rested for a moment on the number plate of the Fiat estate car – JKY 384 L.

The door nearest to the car was painted a glossy purple and a brass figure 3 glinted on its surface. Harry walked towards it, his rubber-soled shoes making no sound on the flat cobblestones. The door was ajar, the interior in pitch darkness.

An instinct developed during years of police work forbade him to walk straight through a doorway into darkness with the light behind him. Standing at the hinged side he pushed the door open till it swung back against the wall behind. The small hallway was empty, offering no cover where anyone might hide. Ahead a deeply carpeted flight of stairs led upward to a small landing where a subdued orange light glowed faintly. The stairway was inviting and hospitable, encouraging the visitor to feel at home as soon as he entered the street door.

Harry went up the stairs slowly, feeling the pile of the carpet cushioning his steps. The door of Peter Newton's flat was on the right at the top. From overhead a recessed ceiling light shed a pool of brightness on the carpet – and incidentally on anyone standing outside the door. The door itself was white, the beading picked out in gold paint. Beside it, inserted in a brass frame, was Peter Newton's visiting card. Below was a bell push.

Harry pressed it. Inside the flat a set of chimes sounded discreetly.

Half a minute passed. Harry wondered whether he was being inspected through the one-way peep-hole he had spotted in the door. If the flat was close carpeted he would not have heard the sound of approaching footsteps.

He pressed the bell again, this time more insistently. The chimes repeated their refrain three times. Even from out here Harry thought he could detect a faint whiff of perfume.

There was no knocker. After another twenty seconds he put his finger on the bell and kept it there till the carillon sounded like a summons to some mysterious form of black mass.

Somewhere outside a car door was closed. Not banged, but firmly closed. Harry looked at his watch. 10.35. He would wait for Peter Newton in the comfort of his own car.

He was just turning away when from inside the flat came a new sound. The telephone had started to ring. Harry paused, waiting to see if anyone answered it.

The caller was insistent. The bell continued ringing in the empty flat for a good three minutes before it stopped. As always the effect was one of mystery and vacuum, as all contact with the person at the other end was irrevocably lost.

Thoughtfully Harry went down the stairs.

The mews outside was still deserted. He stood at the doorway, staring towards the Fiat. A patch of colour on the ground by the rear passenger door had caught his attention. He walked across to the Fiat, bent down and picked up the scarf. It was a flimsy, colourful piece of nylon organza, the sort of thing that women wear in cars to keep their hair in place.

Harry put it to his nose. The scent was strong, but he could not be sure that it was the same as he had noticed outside Peter Newton's flat.

At that moment the warning signals began to sound in Harry's brain. He felt the back of his scalp prickling. In the rear of the estate car a rug had been thrown over an oddly-shaped bundle.

He went round to the tail-gate of the Fiat, got out his handkerchief so that he could operate the handle without blurring any fingerprints that might be on it. It was not locked and swung open easily.

Harry pulled the rug up gingerly. Underneath was a golf-bag, a trolley and a leather grip containing a change of clothing. With a sense of relief he pulled the rug back into place, covering a set of golfing gear that must have been worth over a hundred pounds.

He closed the tail-gate and moved round to the door by the passenger's seat. The window was half lowered. On the seat lay an open packet of cigarettes and an evening newspaper. After a moment's thought he threw the scarf on to the seat beside them.

It was nearly 10.40. Newton was damnably unpunctual. As he strolled back to his own car Harry lit one of his rare cigarettes. He was not a chain_ smoker but he carried cigarettes for occasions such as this. A good cigarette killed impatience, made the tedium of waiting more tolerable.

The seat on the passenger's side, unencumbered by the steering-wheel and pedals was always a more comfortable place to sit during these vigils, with which he was all too, familiar. He was still looking back at the Fiat when he opened the door of his own car.

Something heavy leaning against the door forced it open against his hand. The object slumped out, thudding heavily against the lower frame of the door. Looking down Harry found himself staring into the upside-down face of Peter Newton. His mouth was wide open, his eyes staring.

His body had been shoved across the front seats of the Austin 1100, the doubled up legs jammed against one door, the head against the other. Relieved of the pressure the lifeless body was slowly stretching itself out as the weight of the head and shoulders slithered down on to the cobblestones.

*

'This girl – the girl you saw with Newton this morning – would you recognise her again?'

Chief Superintendent Hal Yardley's voice was ominously friendly and quiet. It was the kind of tone a grandparent uses to a small child. Harry knew that it was usually the prelude to one of Yardley's 'rockets'.

'Yes, I would.'

'Okay. Go on, Dawson.'

'Well,' Harry said uncomfortably, 'as soon as I realised that the car number was the same, I telephoned Newton and made an appointment to see him.'

'Why?'

There was no answer to that question which would satisfy Yardley and Harry knew it. He was sitting beside his Chief in a car without police markings, which was parked at the side of Linton Close. Barely twenty minutes had passed since he had telephoned Nat Fletcher at Scotland Yard, but the mews was already un-recognisable as the quiet backwater into which Harry had driven at 10.30.

Half a dozen police vehicles had moved into the narrow street. Uniformed constables were keeping back the onlookers who had crowded round the entrance from Kennerton Street, trying to con-trol the photographers and newsmen who had been on the scene almost as rapidly as the police. A brilliant arc-light had been set up to illuminate the area round the Austin 1100. Inside the screen which had been erected to hide the car and its macabre contents the police doctor was just completing his preliminary examina-tion. Fingerprint men and plain-clothes detectives were quietly but swiftly going about their business. The police ambulance was just starting to reverse into the mews to transport the body to the police mortuary where it would be subjected to detailed examina-tion by the pathologist and forensic experts.

Harry knew that he could also say goodbye to his own car for some time. It would be taken away and subjected to as minute an examination as the corpse.

'Why?' Yardley repeated his question. It was like the sharp

clap of thunder which presages a storm. Harry made up his mind that he was not going to react as if he were an erring schoolboy.

'I wanted to question him.'

'You wanted to question him.' Yardley seemed to have difficulty in believing his ears. 'You were fully aware that he was under investigation by Divisional CID and yet you took it upon yourself to—'

'With respect, sir,' Harry interrupted, staring straight ahead through the windscreen. 'I was not acting officially.'

'No? Then how the hell were you acting?'

'As a son, sir. A son whose father has just been killed. You see, it's my belief – my firm belief – that Newton in fact knew my father.' Harry turned to face the Superintendent's angry stare. 'I don't believe my father was killed accidentally, sir.'

'I don't know about your father. But we do know Newton was shot in the back of the head by a small calibre pistol.' The shaggy eyebrows lowered and joined in a frown. 'The way I heard it, Dawson, you'd been jumping to all sorts of premature conclusions about this character Newton. And now here you are making an appointment to see him this evening without even—'

'I've told you why I made the appointment,' Harry said with mounting exasperation. Nat Fletcher had emerged from behind the screen and was coming towards the car. He somehow had the look of a man who bears ill tidings. 'I made that appointment because I was curious. It seemed very odd that my father should have written down the number of Newton's car, when—'

Harry stopped. He had lost Yardley's interest. The Chief Superintendent had lowered his window to hear what Nat had to say.

'Yes. What is it, Nat?'

'There's no sign of the gun,' Nat said. 'It might still be in the mews but we've searched it pretty thoroughly. We're going up to the flat now.'

'Okay.'

Nat glanced uncomfortably at Harry and then handed Yardley a slip of paper. 'We found this on Newton, sir. It was in his waistcoat pocket.'

With another glance at Harry, Nat moved away. Yardley twisted round so that the light from the arc-lamp fell on the small rectangle of flimsy paper. He scrutinised it for a few moments then directed a strange look at Harry.

'When you spoke to Newton on the phone, Dawson, did he say anything about a letter?'

'A letter?'

'Yes.'

'No.' Harry shook his head. 'Why should he?'

'Apparently he sent you a letter – a registered letter. He posted it today. Here's the receipt.'

Reluctantly Harry took the receipt. His own name and address had been entered in black Post Office biro.

'Have you any idea what was in that letter?'

'No, not the slightest.'

'You're sure?'

'Of course, I'm sure!' Harry snapped in a tone quite unsuitable for addressing a superior officer.

Well, don't worry,' Yardley replied with surprising mildness. 'We'll know tomorrow morning, Dawson. We'll both know.'

Harry found it impossible to sleep once daylight had come. He could not take his mind from the thought of the registered letter going through all the processes of the Post Office and probably already in some postman's delivery satchel Still in his pyjamas and dressing-gown he had cooked himself breakfast and this time had tried to get some semblance of order into the kitchen when he had finished.

At half-past eight he went out of the flat and down to the street door to see whether the mail had come. Registered letters some-times did not arrive till a later delivery. There was no mail, but the morning paper lay on the mat inside the door. Harry picked it up, opened the door on to the street and left it like that so that the postman could come right up to the flat.

The morning paper carried a ghoulish picture of the murder scene in Linton Close with an inset showing a head and shoulders portrait of Peter Newton.

Harry had just reached the landing when the sound of a heavy tread on the stairs behind him made him turn round. The imposing form of Chief Superintendent Yardley was just starting to ascend.

'Am I too early for you?' Yardley said. For such a heavy man he had come up the stairs with remarkable rapidity and ease. Harry assumed that the remark was intended as a veiled rebuke for his still being in his pyjamas.

'No,' he said standing aside. 'Come along in.'

'Has the post been?'

'Not yet. It should be here any minute.'

Yardley walked into the sitting-room, his eyes automatically making a professional survey of the visible portion of the Dawson flat.

'Would you like some coffee? I was just going to make myself a cup.'

'Not for me.' Yardley swung round, gazing blandly into Harry's eyes. 'But you go ahead.'

'There was no need to call round, sir,' Harry said, meeting the older man's stare. 'I'd have delivered the letter to you.'

'Yes, I know that. But I wanted to see you.' Yardley nodded at the most comfortable of the leather-covered chairs. May I sit down?'

'Yes, of course.'

While the cushions of the chair sighed under the weight of Yardley's mammoth posterior, Harry perched himself on the arm of the settee.

'Go ahead. Make your coffee.'

'That's all right. The coffee can wait. I've plenty of time. I'm on leave anyway.'

'Ah, yes,' Yardley nodded, as if this was news to him. 'Until when?'

'The twenty-fifth. What was it you wanted to see me about?'

Again Yardley contemplated Harry for a moment before speaking. His mouth had a curious way of twitching at the corners when he was about to say something.

'Dawson, you told me last night that you had never met Newton – not until you saw him on the golf course.'

'That's right.'

The next question was fired suddenly, like a slow bowler unexpectedly flinging down a fast ball. 'Then how about a man called Higgs. Do you know anyone of that name?'

'Higgs? No, I don't think so.'

Yardley felt in his pocket and drew out his wallet. 'The full name is Basil Higgs.'

'Basil?' Harry stood up. He had remembered the name now. 'I made out a cheque to a man called Basil Higgs yesterday morning.'

'That's right.' Yardley produced the cheque from his pocket. 'You did indeed, Dawson. A cheque for five pounds.'

Harry took the cheque which Yardley handed him. 'Where did you get this cheque?'

'We found it, last night.'

'Where?'

'In a drawer in Peter Newton's flat.'

'But – I didn't give it to Newton!'

'I'm quite prepared to believe that since it is made out to a Mr. Basil Higgs,' Yardley conceded equably.

'Yes, but I didn't give it to Higgs either. You see I – let me explain.'

'I wish you would,' said Yardley with feeling.

Briefly Harry described the saga of Zero, how the Conways had seen the advertisement and telephoned to say they had found the dog.

'I drove over there yesterday morning to pick him up. They seemed very nice people. He's an invalid. Has to get about in a wheelchair. Anyway, when I was leaving I mentioned the reward and Arnold Conway suggested that I give the fiver to some pet charity of his. He asked me to make the cheque out to the secretary, Basil Higgs.'

'I see.' Yardley stretched out an arm to take the cheque. He replaced it in his wallet which he put in his pocket. 'Then how did Newton get hold of it?'

'I don't know.' Harry shook his head in complete bewilderment. 'I just can't imagine.'

The two men were staring at each other in silence when there came a sharp knock on the street door, followed by a peal of the bell.

'Is that the postman?' Yardley had begun to rise expectantly from his chair.

'Most probably.'

Harry went out into the hall and opened the door to the landing. The postman had just reached the top of the stairs and was standing there with a bundle of letters. Against the top one he was holding the registered letter receipt book.

'Mornin'.'

'Good morning.'

'Registered letter for Dawson. Sign here, please.'

Harry signed his name with the postman's pencil and accepted the long bulky envelope which was handed to him. 'Thank you.'

'Thankin' *you*, sir,' the postman replied cheerfully, as the door closed.

Harry put the bundle of mail down on the hall table and, holding the registered envelope in his hand, walked slowly back into the sitting-room.

'Has it arrived?' Yardley could not conceal his impatience. 'Yes.'

Still looking at the long, slightly bulging envelope Harry crossed to the desk and picked up his father's letter knife. As he inserted the point under the heavily sealed flap Yardley was at his shoulder.

Harry drew out a single sheet of plain notepaper. It bore no address or date. The message had been printed in rough capitals:

'THIS IS WHY YOUR FATHER WAS KILLED.
PETER NEWTON'

'This is why your father was killed.' Unashamedly Yardley read the message aloud. Harry handed him the sheet and ripped open the side of the envelope. Inside was an object carefully wrapped in tissue paper. Harry undid several layers of the paper before the object inside was revealed. It was an ornate, beautifully made dog collar.

'It's the collar!' Harry exclaimed.

'The collar?'

'Yes. The one that was stolen. The one Zero was wearing.' 'Now, wait a minute,' Yardley protested. 'You're sure this was the one that was on the poodle?'

'Harry turned the stiff leather ring in his hands. 'Yes. I'm sure.'

'Then what the devil does this message mean?'

Yardley's brows met as he frowned over the printed words. 'Search me. It doesn't make sense.'

'All right.' Yardley laid the message down on the desk and nodded at the collar. 'Then tell me about that. Where did it come from, originally?'

'I don't know where it came from. All I can tell you is that my father gave it to Mrs. Rogers for her birthday.'

'When was this?'

'About a month ago. Unfortunately Mrs. Rogers is away at the moment. Her nephew got the 'flu and she's looking after him for a few days.'

Harry laid the collar down on top of the message. 'I wonder what the devil Newton was getting at?'

'So do I. It looks a perfectly ordinary collar to me. A little ornate perhaps.'

Yardley turned away. He seemed to have come to a sudden decision.

'I'd like to see you later this morning, Dawson. Could you be in my office at eleven?'

'Yes,' Harry said, looking at his watch. 'I shall be in the building. They're taking my prints some time this morning.'

'It's routine.' Yardley spoke casually. 'They've been giving your car a thorough going-over, as you probably know.'

While he spoke the bell had been ringing. Not the bell on the street door but the small bell on the door that opened from the flat on to the landing.

Harry slipped past the Chief Superintendent and went to open it. He found Nat Fletcher with his finger poised to give the bell-push another jab. He held a bulging manila envelope in his other hand.

'Hallo, Nat!' Harry greeted his friend guardedly. Since last night he was not too sure which side Nat was on. It was reasonable to believe that duty called him to act in harmony with his Chief Superintendent.

"'Lo, Harry. Is Yardley here?'

'He is. He is indeed. Come along in, Nat.'

Yardley was evidently not expecting Nat to track him down to the Dawson flat.

'Hallo, Nat. What brings you here?'

'Good morning, sir. I've just come from Newton's place. Things are beginning to look interesting.'

'Would you like some coffee, Nat?' Harry offered, hoping to get things on to the old friendly basis.

Nat brushed the invitation aside: 'No, thank you, Harry.'

'What do you mean, interesting?' Yardley demanded.

Nat unbuttoned the showerproof coat he habitually wore.

His face showed the effects of a night without sleep.

'We were just finishing off at the flat when Jackson found a door behind what we thought was a larder. There was a small room, fitted up as an office. Desk, typewriter, filing-cabinet, all the usual office paraphernalia.'

'Well?'

Nat was standing close to the desk on which he had laid the envelope. He had spotted the collar lying on the sheet of note paper. 'We've just spent a fascinating half-hour going through the filing-cabinet, sir – to say nothing of the desk.'

'Get to the point,' Yardley snapped, irritated by Nat's suggestive tone.

'What did you find, Nat?' Harry chipped in.

Nat looked from Harry to the Superintendent and back again. There was a mischievous smile on his face, like a conjurer who knows he is going to surprise his audience.

Suddenly he picked up the envelope and let the contents slip out on to the table in the centre of the room.

There were about fifty glossy photographs and every one of them was of a different girl. Some were nudes, some were semi-nudes, some represented girls in the act of stripping, others showed them in black suspender belts clipped to black stockings. They had been taken from every conceivable angle and the fullest possible use had been made of light to heighten the effect.

In silence Yardley riffled through the collection. His breathing had become a good deal heavier. Nat stood back, enjoying the effect he had created. Harry picked up a photograph of a girl with a brash face and very well-developed bust.

'I know this girl. She's a prostitute. She gave evidence in the Oxford case about six months ago.'

Nat nodded his agreement. 'It's my guess they're all prostitutes, every one of them. There's over two hundred photos in that room, sir.'

'Two hundred.' Yardley was still intent on the selection of fifty which Nat had brought. 'Our friend Newton must have had a very large circle of friends.'

'A very *strange* circle of friends, sir,' Nat corrected. 'No names, no phone numbers, no addresses, no details, of any kind. Just the photographs.'

Yardley scooped the photographs together and pushed them back into the envelope. He handed it back to Nat.

'What the hell was Newton up to, Nat?'

The indoor swimming baths had only recently been opened. They had been built to the most modern standards and offered every conceivable amenity. The main pool was on the Olympic scale and lined on both sides by tiers of benches for spectators. At eleven on a normal weekday morning these were almost empty.

Harry Dawson sat on the front row watching the girl who was just completing her third length in a fast racing crawl. The white bathing cap raised a bow-wave ahead of her and the water rushed over her lithe form. In the confined space voices were echoed and magnified. The air was damp and heavy, laden with a faint smell of chlorine.

The swimmer reached the end of the pool, turned under water with the agility of an eel and immediately increased her speed in a racing finish. This time when she reached the end she let her legs sink and stood up in the water. She placed her hands on the side of the pool, levered herself up until she could place one leg on the top. It was a movement as graceful as a ballet sequence. The moisture gleamed on the curve of her back as she reached for the towel on the bench.

Perhaps sensing Harry's eyes on her she turned and saw him sitting a few yards behind her. She immediately gave him her brilliant smile and walked towards him.

'Hallo, Mr. Dawson.'

'Hallo, Liz.'

She was pulling off her bathing cap as she approached, shaking her hair out into its natural shape.

'I didn't know you came here.'

'I don't normally. Douglas told me this was the place to find you on your day off.'

Her breast was rising and falling as she recovered her breath after the all-out effort of that final length. Harry had never seen Liz in a bathing suit before. He could not help thinking that her well-rounded yet firm and athletic figure was about ten times more seductive than those photographs which Nat Fletcher had found in Peter Newton's flat.

'Did you want to see me about something? Is there trouble at the shop?'

'I wanted to ask you about this.'

Harry produced Zero's collar from his pocket and showed it to her.

'Isn't that Zero's?'

'That is the number one question. Can you identify it?'

Liz wrapped the big towel round her person and took the collar.

'It certainly looks the same. But where did you get it from, Mr. Dawson? I thought you said Zero wasn't wearing a collar when he was found.'

'Don't worry your head about that, Liz. All I want to know is whether that's the same collar my father bought.'

'Yes.' Liz was turning the collar over in her hands. 'The medallion looks a little different, but—'

'What do you mean, it looks different?'

'I thought the medallion seemed a little smaller but—' She shook her head and handed it back to him. 'No, it's the same collar. I'm sure of it.'

Harry put the collar back in his pocket. 'Have you any idea where my father bought it?'

'Yes. He got it from Heaton's pet shop. The one in St. John's Wood. I think it's in Valence Street.'

'Did you suggest Heaton's to him?'

'Yes. We were talking about Mrs. Rogers one morning and your father said he didn't know what on earth to buy her for her birthday. I suggested a collar for Zero.'

A party of school-children, well-disciplined and marshalled by a couple of women teachers, had emerged from the changing-rooms. Harry guessed that at any moment they would be released into the water with screams of delight. He had noticed a café or refreshment room separated from the pool by glass panels.

'Fancy a drink of something? Replace all that energy you've been burning up.'

Liz nodded eagerly. 'Thank you. I'd love a coffee.'

Harry followed her into the café. She led him towards the counter where there were several empty stools. She perched herself on one and rearranged the towel round herself.

'Liz. There's something I've been meaning to ask you,' Harry said, as he slid on to the stool beside her.

Liz turned her large, dark eyes enquiringly towards him. 'You saw a lot of my father. You saw him most days, in fact. Did he ever say anything, or do anything, that –, well, aroused your curiosity at all?'

She hesitated, dropping her eyes. The counter-hand came along at that moment. Harry gave the order, deciding to have the same as Liz. During the interval Liz had made up her mind.

'No. I don't think so.'

'Are you sure?' Harry persisted. He felt confident that some thought had indeed crossed her mind.

'Well—' Liz used a corner of the towel to clear some moisture from her neck. 'There was one incident, but it was nothing. It really wasn't anything important.'

'Tell me about it, Liz.'

Liz coloured slightly, as if assailed by some inner sense of guilt.

'One day last week. I think it was Tuesday. I arrived back from lunch a little early. Your father was in the shop and I think he was a bit surprised to see me. But I really couldn't help overhearing some of the conversation.'

'I'm sure you didn't on purpose,' Harry assured her. 'Who was he talking to?'

'Well, I assumed she was a customer.'

'She?'

'Yes, a tall, dark, very striking woman of about fifty. She was very expensively dressed. Just as I entered the shop I heard your father say: "For God's sake, Sybil, don't be difficult about – " Then he saw me and started talking in a completely different way.'

Two cups of foamy coffee slid on to the counter beside them. Harry placed a 50p coin on the Formica.

'Go on, Liz.'

'That's all. I went into the office and a few minutes later the woman left.'

'Did my father mention her at all – make any comment?'

'Yes.' Liz helped herself to sugar from the bowl on the counter. 'He made a point of telling me that he'd never seen her before. He said she was looking for a special kind of ski jacket.'

'Did you believe him?'

'I – I didn't know whether to believe him or not.' Liz was clearly embarrassed by Harry's interest in the incident. 'It certainly sounded convincing.'

'Did you say anything to Douglas about this?'

'No, of course not,' Liz said with spirit. 'I didn't tell anyone about it. Why should I? It was none of my business.'

Harry nodded in satisfaction and raised his cup as if he were toasting her in champagne.

'Thank you, Liz.'

*

Not having his own car at his disposal, Harry was forced to take a taxi to St. John's Wood. The morning was already well on and he had not the time to travel by bus and underground. One advantage of going by taxi was that the driver found Heaton's shop for him and dropped him right outside the door.

Heaton's pet shop had a narrow frontage but it stretched a long way back. The window was occupied by the cages of all sorts of birds from common or garden finches to exotically plumed African species. Inside were displayed every kind of luxury that the doting owners of household pets might require. One section of the wall was lined with a miniature menagerie – rows of cages containing white mice, rabbits, puppies, kittens, tortoises, monkeys and hamsters. A pungent smell hung in the air. The background noise of chirpings, barking and animal calls of various kinds gave the place an air of festivity.

Harry wandered as far as the middle of the shop where the 'Dogs' Boutique' was on display. The stand contained leads of various lengths and thicknesses, tartan jackets for pampered pekes, and collars to fit the neck of anything from a chihuahua to a doberman pinscher.

Harry was examining the collars when the curtain screening the inner room at the end of the shop parted and the proprietor emerged. He was wiping his lips with a handkerchief and gave the impression that he had just been partaking of a little something.

'Good morning, sir.'

'Good morning. Mr. Heaton?'

Mr. Heaton smiled disarmingly. 'The same.'

It was hard to determine Sidney Heaton's age. His crinkly hair was already silvering and he had run to weight around the stomach. But his facial skin was smooth and rosy and there was a youthful twinkle in his eyes. He wore a spotted bow tie and a belted jacket with four patch pockets.

'Were you interested in something for a doggie?'

'I'm a police officer, Mr. Heaton – from Scotland Yard – and I'm making a few enquiries. I think perhaps you may be able to help me.'

'Oh, dear!' Heaton's eyes ran anxiously round the rows of cages as if he were wondering which of his pets had been so indiscreet as to get on the wrong side of the law. 'Well, if I can I will certainly, my dear sir.'

Harry had produced Zero's collar from his pocket and Heaton's eyes had fastened uneasily on it.

'What is it you are making enquiries about?'

'About this collar. I understand my father – Tom Dawson – bought it from you about—'

'Are you Mr. Dawson's son?' Heaton's whole manner had changed. He looked at Harry as if he had found a long lost friend.

'Yes. I am.'

'Oh, Mr. Dawson, I'm delighted to meet you!' With equal swiftness his expression changed to one of concern. 'But I was so distressed to hear about your father. What a dreadful thing to have happened!'

'Thank you, Mr. Heaton. Did you know my father?'

No – but we met, of course, when he bought the collar. I'd been an admirer of his for years. I was very thrilled when he came into my shop that afternoon. You'll find it hard to believe, Mr. Dawson, but I was quite an athlete myself in the old days.'

Heaton looked down sadly at his generous stomach.

"Mr. Heaton, I want you to take a look at this collar. Firstly, is it the one you sold my father and secondly is there anything unusual about it?'

Heaton took the now much handled dog collar and examined it with professional interest.

'Yes, this is the collar I sold your father – so far as I can tell.'

'So far as you can tell?'

Heaton smiled. 'Well, I've sold quite a few like this and they all look very much alike, of course.' He waved a well-manicured hand at the display stand. 'As you see, I have quite a stock of them at the moment. Some are a little more decorative than others perhaps, but they're all more or less the same.'

He picked a collar from its hook and held it beside Zero's.

42

'I don't think there's anything unusual about your one, Mr. Dawson.'

'What about the medallion? Is that the same one or has it been changed?'

Heaton's brows furrowed as he made an effort of recollection. 'You realise, of course, that I didn't supply this particular medallion. Your father brought it with him.'

'He *brought* it?'

'Yes.' Heaton stopped and struck his brow with the palm of his hand. 'No ! No, I'm terribly sorry. I've just remembered. His friend brought it. That's right. Your father was just trying to make up his mind whether to buy the collar or not, and then his friend arrived. She said it was absolutely perfect and just the thing he wanted.'

'And she brought the medallion?'

Heaton nodded. 'That's right. She took it out of her handbag and I fitted it to the collar. They were both highly delighted.'

Harry put out his hand and Heaton gave the collar back to him. 'Was the name and address already on the medallion or did you put it on?'

'No, no. It was already on.'

In the background one of the monkeys had started an excited jabbering. The mood spread along the cages and one of the smaller puppies began to whimper in alarm.

Harry had to raise his voice to make himself heard. 'Who was this friend of my father's? Did you know her?'

'No. I'm afraid not.'

'Was she a rather short, plump woman with a belligerent expression?'

'Oh, dear me no!' Heaton said, bridling. 'She seemed a very charming lady.'

'Tall, dark, very elegantly dressed?'

'Expensively dressed, certainly. Somewhat distastefully, though, to anyone of – shall we say, sensibility.'

'I don't follow you, Mr. Heaton.'

Heaton moved to the nearest of the cages and put his fingers through the bars to caress a marmoset monkey, which pressed itself against his hand appreciatively.

'Not that I'm one of your conservationist cranks or anything, you understand. Oh, dear me, no. But, working with animals so much one develops a certain affinity over the years, don't you know. An affinity.'

Heaton dwelt on the word, pleased to have found the right expression. There was an almost boyish frankness on his face.

'And then a woman comes in with a leopard-skin coat draped carelessly over her shoulders and – well, it makes one's hackles rise a bit.'

He laughed at himself deprecatingly and withdrew his hand from the cage.

'Is that what she was wearing? Leopard skin?'

'In fact it was – er, what do you call them? Ocelot. Yes, that's right, ocelot.'

Harry was beginning to move towards the door, the collar safely back in his pocket.

'Well, thank you, Mr. Heaton, you've been most helpful.' Still anxious to please, Heaton hurried past him to hold the door.

'Thank you, sir. I do hope we shall meet again, Mr. Dawson.'

From a shelf behind him a Siamese cat sprang and landed on Heaton's shoulder. Its blue eyes rested on Harry with an expression of implacable hostility totally at variance with its master's bland smile.

Superintendent Yardley had done what he could to humanise the very modem office which he had been allocated when Scotland Yard had been moved from its old home on the Embankment to the new building in Victoria Street. Yet the ancient partners' desk and the well-worn leather easy chairs seemed just a little out of place here and the pastoral landscape from his favourite Breughel painting made a sharp contrast to the bustling scene in Victoria Street fifty feet below his window. Much of the end wall was occupied by a large-scale map of the Metropolitan Police area, studded by pins with round coloured heads.

A small secretarial office had been built into the rectangular space, its door opening off the corridor which its own wall formed. A uniformed clerk emerged from this office as Harry entered.

'Hallo, Hodges. The Chief Superintendent anywhere about?'

'He hasn't returned from Hampstead yet, sir.'

'Hampstead?'

'Yes, sir. He told me he'd be going out there this morning.'

'All right, Hodges.' Harry nodded in satisfaction. He was glad that Yardley would get personal confirmation of his story. He moved on into the spacious office. 'By the way, is Inspector Fletcher in the building?'

Hodges nodded towards a communicating door which led into the neighbouring office. 'I think he's in the other office, sir. Shall I tell him you're here?'

Before Hodges could reach the communicating door it opened and Nat appeared.

'Ah, Nat!' Harry greeted him and hurried on impatiently. 'Did you get anything from Carter yet? The post-mortem findings? The forensic report?'

'Hold it, Harry.' Nat put up a defensive hand to halt the barrage of questions. 'I've had my own little murder to worry about, you know.'

The look of anger and frustration on Harry's face was unmistakable. Hodges retreated tactfully to the outer office.

Nat put a friendly hand on the younger man's shoulder. 'However, I understand Carter and his chief are officially treating your father's death as a case of murder.'

Harry grunted. 'He could hardly do anything else, With the prime suspect getting himself shot in the head.'

'No.' Nat looked down at the photograph he was holding in his hand. 'Anyway, à propos of Newton, suppose you just take a decco at this.'

Harry glanced down at the snapshot which Nat handed him. It was a smallish, glossy colour print and it showed Peter Newton and a very shapely girl lying on sunbathing mats at the side of a swimming pool. They were grinning at the camera and obviously in holiday mood.

'Do you recognise her?'

'Yes.' Harry's eyes were still fixed on the face of the girl, which seemed to be directing its smile to him personally. It was an attractive face and he felt an irrational sense of outrage at a girl like that being in the company of a man such as Newton, and apparently enjoying it. 'She's the girl I told you about. The one he was having a row with in the car I saw on the Finchley Road.'

'I was hoping you'd say that.' Nat removed the photo from Harry's fingers.

'But who is she?'

'Her name's Judy Black. She's been living with Newton. Last night they had dinner together at a place in Charlotte Street. Apparently they had a flaming row there too and left the restaurant together at about half-past nine.'

'Have you picked her up yet?'

'Not yet.'

'Why not, for Pete's sake?' Harry protested.

'Why not? My God, you sound just like Yardley.'

Nat sat himself down in one of his Chief's leather armchairs and crossed his legs.

'Because we can't find her, Harry. That's why not.'

Harry paced restlessly across the room. From the small office came the sound of Hodges' tentative typing.

'Did she go back to the flat with Newton?'

'We don't know. That's what we're trying to find out.'

'Where does this girl come from? What's her background?'

'She's from Liverpool.' In his turn Nat was appreciatively studying the bikini-clad girl in the photograph. 'Apparently Newton saw her in a show there and persuaded her to come to Town. He got her a part in some musical – the one at the St. Edward's – and it flopped. Until about a month ago she was in digs near Notting Hill Gate, then she moved in with Newton.'

Harry looked at his friend more approvingly. It was clear that Nat had not been idle.

'Who told you all this?'

'Her ex-landlady.'

'And what about Newton?'

'We're not making any headway, I'm afraid. No one wants to talk about him. All we know is that he had a private income and backed one or two shows in the West End, including the flop Judy Black was in. Anyway, I've told Sergeant Quilter to snoop around. He usually comes up with something.'

'Nat, whatever happens, you've got to find that girl!'

'Don't worry, I'll find—'

Nat broke off and rapidly got to his feet. The office door had opened and Yardley was bustling in.

'Sorry to have kept you, Harry. I've been out to Hampstead.'

He put his brief-case on the desk and turned to Nat. 'Any news? Have you picked the girl up yet?'

'No. Not yet, sir.' Nat held up the snapshot. 'But Harry identified her. She *was* the girl in the car with Newton. And the landlady now thinks—'

'I don't want to hear any more about the landlady,' Yardley said curtly, moving round to the back of his desk. 'I want that girl, Judy Black. Find her!'

Nat was dismissed. Swallowing his resentment he went out quickly through the communicating door. Yardley deposited his weight on the swivel chair behind his desk. His eyes swung up to Harry and then dropped again.

'Sit down, Dawson.'

Harry sat down in the slightly warm chair which Nat had vacated. Yardley picked up a typed foolscap sheet from his desk and frowned at it. There was silence in the office for a full minute. In the background could be heard the irregular murmur of the traffic in Victoria Street, the tap of Hodges' typewriter and the ringing of telephone bells in nearby offices.

Still studying the report, Yardley spoke suddenly. 'I've seen the Conways this morning.'

'Yes. I thought perhaps you had.'

'They confirm your story about the dog.'

47

'I'm pleased to hear it,' Harry said drily. 'Did you expect they wouldn't?'

Yardley laid the typewritten sheet down, leaned his forearms on the desk and fixed Harry with his formidable stare.

'As a matter of fact I was lucky to catch the Conways. They were just off to Aldeburgh, where he is apparently a member of the golf club.'

Harry was about to say something when he remembered that some clubs have associate as well as playing members.

'They're a very civil couple.' Yardley's expression became less hard as he remembered the flattering courtesy which Sybil Conway had shown him.

'Yes, I thought so too,' Harry agreed.

'However,' Yardley continued, 'neither Mr. nor Mrs. Conway have any recollection of you giving them a cheque for five pounds and they have certainly no knowledge of anyone named Basil Higgs.'

For a few moments Harry was unable to find words. 'But – didn't he tell you about the Hamsters?'

'You certainly made me look a fool there, Dawson. Polite though they were they had to laugh when I mentioned the Hamsters. In fact, Arnold Conway was laughing so much that he tripped over his own rug.'

'Wait a minute.' Something in the picture which Yardley's account had conjured up was all wrong. 'How could a man in a wheelchair trip over a rug?'

'Conway wasn't in a wheelchair. When I asked him about it he was completely flabbergasted. The man's as fit as a fiddle.'

'But—'

'Just to make sure,' Yardley ploughed on, called in on an old friend of mine, Inspector Emerson. He knows Hampstead better than you know your flat, Dawson. He should do, he's been there for twenty years.'

Harry stared at Yardley's face. He just could not believe that this conversation was actually happening. The room, the desk, the Chief Superintendent himself had suddenly become quite unreal, like symbols in a dream.

'Emerson told me that Conway was a stock-broker who had made his pile and retired. He bought Stillwater in 1963 and paid thirty thousand for it. I also mentioned the wheelchair. Conway may be getting on but he hasn't reached the bath-chair stage yet. In fact, he plays squash twice a week and golf on Sundays.'

Harry sprang up from the chair and strode over to the window. 'I don't care whether he plays tennis, squash, golf or ice-hockey. He was in a wheelchair when I saw him yester-day.'

He turned angrily towards the Chief Superintendent. 'Good God, why should I invent a thing like that if it wasn't true?'

Yardley's answer was so quiet that it was almost inaudible. 'I can't imagine why.'

Harry moved round to the edge of the desk and leaned down on it. 'You don't believe me, do you?'

Yardley did not answer. Instead he opened a top drawer and took from it Zero's collar.

'Tell me about this collar. Did you find out anything?'

Harry got a hold of his temper with difficulty. 'It was bought by my father from a shop in St. John's Wood. There's doubt, a slight doubt, about the medallion.'

'You mean it might have been changed?'

Yardley turned the metal disc over between his finger and thumb. 'It's got Mrs. Rogers' name on it and your phone number.'

'Yes. But both Liz Mason and the man who owns the pet shop, his name's Heaton, were a little doubtful.'

Harry stopped as a knock sounded on the communicating door and Nat thrust it open.

'Can you spare a moment, sir?'

'Yes. What is it, Nat?'

Nat glanced at Harry's face, saw that it was flushed with anger and guessed that he had interrupted an angry session.

'I've just had a call from Sergeant Quilter. He's found out something about Newton, sir, something we didn't know.'

'Well?' Yardley barked, irritated by Nat's habit of preluding his big announcements with these mysterious remarks.

'His name wasn't Peter Newton, that's just a name he used because he thought his own conveyed the wrong image for the world of show business. His real name is Higgs, sir, Basil Higgs.'

It was late afternoon when Harry got home. He had lunched in the canteen at Scotland Yard, hoping that he would be able to collect his car soon afterwards, when the experts had finished their examination of it. In the end it was around four when he was at last told that it was available and consequently he was caught up in the beginnings of the rush-hour. As he parked opposite the flat he noticed a taxi drawn up outside the shop.

His nerves and temper were in a raw state as he turned the key in the lock of the street entrance to the flat. He had just closed it behind him when he realised that someone was coming out on to the landing at the top of the stairs. He stood still in the dark shadow just inside 'the door.

Mrs. Rogers was wearing her tweed coat and the hat with plastic flowers on it. She was so absorbed with the poodle in her arms that she did not notice Harry. She was pouching out her lips to the animal, receiving a thorough licking on the mouth and nose.

Half way down the stairs she spotted Harry and halted in obvious embarrassment.

'Good evening, Mrs. Rogers,' said Harry blandly.

'Oh ! Oh, hallo, Mr. Dawson.' She forced a smile. 'I – I was hoping to see you.'

'Were you, Mrs. Rogers? I find that a little difficult to believe. I trust your nephew's fully recovered from the 'flu by now?'

'Oh, yes, Mr. Dawson, thank you. He is.' She came down a few more steps. The coldness in Harry's tone had been unmistakable. 'Mr. Dawson, I'm afraid I owe you an apology. I lied to you in that note I left for you. The fact of the matter is, I've got another job.'

'Oh?'

'Yes. At that new hotel in Knightsbridge. The Royal Plaza.'

'All a bit sudden, isn't it?'

Harry moved to one side as she reached the bottom of the

stairs. She had pushed the poodle across her left breast and it was now engaged in laundering her left ear.

'I just didn't know what to do. The shock of your father dying like that. Well, I just had to get away. I'm afraid I behaved very badly, Mr. Dawson. I don't want to appear ungrateful for all your kindness but – I'm really very sorry about it.'

She seemed thoroughly ashamed of herself but Harry suspected that the whole show was an act.

'How much do I owe you?' he said, to cut short her protestations.

'Nothing,' she said quickly. 'Nothing at all, thank you. We're all square, with you paying the reward.'

Harry knew this was not true but he let it pass. 'Well, anyway, we found your dog for you.'

'Yes. And you can imagine how thrilled I was when I heard about it. I just couldn't believe it.' She fondled the dog's ears. 'Dear little Zero.'

'How did you hear about it, Mrs. Rogers?' Harry made no attempt to move away from the door and until he did she could not reach the latch.

'I spoke to Hubert this afternoon and he told me about it. By the way, what's happened to Zero's collar, Mr. Dawson? Was it stolen?'

'Yes.'

'Oh, dear.' She turned the corners of her mouth down. 'It was such a lovely little collar. And it was a birthday present from your father too, you know.'

'Curiously enough,' Harry said carefully, watching her face, 'it was both stolen *and* returned.'

'Returned?'

'Yes. At the moment Superintendent Yardley's got it.' 'Superintendent Yardley?' Mrs. Roger's repeated the name in alarm. 'But why on earth have the police got it?'

Harry was spared having to answer by an angry tattoo on the door knocker. He opened the door to find an impatient taxi-driver standing there.

'Look. I can't wait here all night, lady. I shall be in trouble, real trouble, if you don't get a move on.'

'I'll be with you in a minute.'

'Now, *please*, lady.' He nodded towards the street and looked at Harry. 'There's a busy-body of a traffic warden out there. She's a real stinker!'

The driver turned back to his cab. Harry half closed the door. 'Mrs. Rogers, before you go there's something I want to ask you. Did you ever hear my father mention the name Conway?'

'Conway?' Her face had gone blank. 'No, I don't think so.'

'You've never heard the name before?'

'No I haven't.' She shook her head vigorously. 'I feel sure I would have remembered if your father had mentioned it at all. Mr. Dawson, you'll have to excuse me.'

She was peering out into the street, where the taxi-driver had started up his engine.

'All right, Mrs. Rogers. Goodbye and good luck with the new job.'

She gave him a shamefaced smile. 'Thank you. Say goodbye to Mr. Dawson, Zero.'

Zero ignored the suggestion, to Harry's relief. He stood back and watched her as she hurried across the pavement and got into the taxi. Although she had had the run of the flat for months it somehow made him feel uneasy to think that she had been prowling about up there alone today of all days.

Harry had only meant to take a cat-nap when he sat down in the comfortable arm-chair. But a sleepless night followed by the stresses of his two encounters with Yardley had taken their toll. His head dropped and his eyes closed.

The telephone bell startled him into wakefulness. He shook his head, trying to remember what time it was. Outside it had grown dark and the din of traffic had diminished to a murmur.

He stumbled to his feet, clawing at the standard lamp to switch on some light. He blinked at the face of his watch. It was seven minutes to ten. He had been asleep for five hours.

Fortunately the caller was persistent. The bell still continued its regular ringing tone. Still rather befuddled by the effects of an unplanned sleep he grabbed up the instrument.

'586 2679.'

Instead of a reply came the series of pips which indicated that the call was coming through a coin-box. Harry waited.

'Mr. Dawson?' The voice was a woman's, low-pitched, breathless and nervous.

'Yes, speaking.'

'This is Judy Black, Mr. Dawson. I was a friend of Mr. Newton's—'

'Judy Black !'

'I'm in trouble, Mr. Dawson,' the girl rushed on. She had a faint North Country accent, but he thought it sounded more like Leeds than Liverpool. 'Terrible trouble, and I'd like to talk to you before I give myself up. Can we meet some time? Tonight, if possible.'

'Yes, of course.' Harry reached for a note-pad and biro. 'Where are you? Where are you speaking from?'

The girl did not answer at once. The vague background sounds he had heard were blanked out, as if she had covered the mouth-piece with her hand. After a few moments she spoke again, very quietly and swiftly.

'I'm in a restaurant. The Chez Maurice. It's in Greek Street. The top end, near Soho Square.'

'Stay where you are, Miss Black.' Harry spoke in his most authoritative police officer's voice. All his sleepiness had vanished. 'I'll be with you in fifteen minutes.'

The taxi cruised slowly up Greek Street. Both Harry and the driver were looking for some sign that would indicate the whereabouts of Chez Maurice.

Suddenly Harry spotted the name on the right-hand side of the street. He rapped on the glass partition. 'There it is! Stop here.'

'Can't stop here, mate. I'll pull into that gap up there.'

Harry could clearly see the two girls who were standing under the lights that illuminated the entrance. They had just come out and were thinking about hailing a cab. The taller of the two was a robustly built woman of about thirty. She was attractive in a tough, no-nonsense kind of way. Her red hair caught the light from the neon strip above.

The girl beside her was a real stunner. Men passing by were slowing down, instinctively running their eyes over her. Harry recognised her at once as the girl he had seen in the Fiat.

Harry already had the door of the cab open as it pulled in to the kerb thirty yards farther on. He waited impatiently while the driver fumbled for change, never taking his eyes off the entrance to Chez Maurice.

Judy Black was alone now. The other girl had gone back into the restaurant, obviously to collect something she had forgotten. Judy was looking nervously up and down the street. It was eighteen minutes since Harry had put the phone down. She must be wondering whether he was going to come.

As the taxi moved away he saw her grope in her handbag and put on a pair of dark glasses. She rearranged her head-scarf in the hope that it might conceal the head of golden hair. He hurried along the pavement, knowing that she had seen his taxi stop and watched him getting out.

A stream of cars and taxis prevented him from crossing. He gave her a nod and a wave which were meant to be reassuring. They had the opposite effect She twisted her head and took a quick look into the restaurant. There was still no sign of her friend. Then, after another anxious glance at Harry, she abruptly came down the two steps to pavement level and started running towards Soho Square.

Something had scared her or she had changed her mind about talking to him. He plunged into the road, handing off a sharply braking sports car and squeezing- through the ten-inch gap between it and the car in front. Judy had a start of twenty yards as he set off after her at the double.

Opposite Chez Maurice the driver of a green mini-van started his engine and forced his way out into the stream of traffic moving towards Soho Square. His speed was just about the same as the two running figures.

A big pre-war Rolls-Royce seven seater Sedanca had stopped

opposite the entrance to a night-spot proclaimed in neon signs as 'The Mad House'. Just before Harry came abreast of it the doors opened and out poured half a dozen long-haired youths in studded jeans. Each of them was carrying a musical instrument, the largest of them a double-bass in an enormous case. They were already fairly high and seemed amused by Harry's efforts to get past them.

One of them grabbed his arm, laughing. 'Say, man, you want to relax! Why not come in with us and we'll smooth you out?'

Harry had to make a big effort to wrench his arm free from the thin but astonishingly strong fingers. In doing so he cannoned into a middle-aged American couple who were surveying, wide-eyed, this piece of local colour. He sent the woman's handbag flying.

He recovered it from the gutter and with minimal apologies returned it to its owner. When he resumed his pursuit Judy Black had disappeared.

Harry raced towards Soho Square, not noticing the mini-van which had passed him and which he now repassed in his turn. He entered the square just in time to see a taxi at the far end turn in to pick up a girl who was waving frantically. Her cry. 'Taxi! Taxi!' was like a desperate call for help.

Realising that he could never reach them in time, Harry halted and watched. The girl climbed aboard and the taxi moved on up the short section of street to Oxford Street. There it turned right. The mini-van accelerated to follow it.

Harry stood hesitating for a moment. An instinct told him that Judy would head back towards the West End. He decided to chance his luck. In any case there was nothing else he could do.

Moving really fast now he sprinted round the square to the opening of Stratton Street. It cut through to Charing Cross Road. He still had a chance to catch Judy's taxi at St. Giles's circus.

He covered the hundred yards or so in fifteen seconds, most of it on. the roadway. Heads turned at the sight of an apparently sane young man who had suddenly gone berserk. Some joker even shouted 'stop thief!'

Traffic was streaming up Charing Cross Road. Harry had to

get to the farther side. Like a rugger player weaving through the New Zealand defence he zigzagged his way through the lethal stream.

Once on the pavement he stood, breathing deeply to recover his breath, his eyes scrutinising the occupants of every taxi that passed. Fifteen private cars and half a dozen taxis went by and then Harry saw a vehicle with a pale-faced girl in-dark glasses on the back seat.

He moved out on to the roadway and held up his hand. The driver could not pass without running him down. For a moment Harry thought he was going to do just that. At the last moment he braked and managed to stop an inch from the immobile figure.

He put his head out of the window. 'What's the game? Haven't you got eyes in your head? Can't you see this cab's taken?'

Harry had moved round beside him. 'I'm a police officer,' he said quietly but with authority. 'Detective Inspector Dawson. I want you to take us directly to Scotland Yard.'

As the driver gaped, Harry wrenched the cab door open and stepped inside. Judy Black, taken completely by surprise, was trying to open the door and jump out on the other side. Harry grabbed her and forced her back on to the seat. He slammed the door and shouted to the cabbie.

'Drive on!'

Still marvelling, the driver engaged his gear and moved on.

Behind him the mini-van, which had endured the hold-up with patience, kept station at a distance of twenty yards.

Harry had sat down on one of the tip-up seats with his back to the driver. That way he could face the frightened girl on the seat opposite. At close quarters she was disquietingly attractive.

'Now,' he demanded angrily. 'What is this? What the hell are you trying to pull?'

'Who are you?' She was literally shaking with fright and the cigarette which she had just lit had fallen from her fingers on to the carpet. 'What do you want of me?'

'You know damn well who I am! I'm Harry Dawson. Inspector Dawson, if you like. You phoned me twenty minutes ago—'

'I – I did?' The girl's voice was- incredulous.

'Why, yes!'

Judy shook her head. 'No. I never phoned you . . .'

'You said you were in bad trouble and wanted to see me—'

Harry stopped. The voice *was* different. There was more Lancashire than Yorkshire in this girl's accent. He picked up the smouldering cigarette, wound the window down and threw it out.

'What you're saying is that it wasn't you on the phone?' Again she shook her head. 'Did someone really phone you, pretending to be me?'

'Yes.'

'It was a tip-off,' Judy said tensely. 'They knew I was at the restaurant.'

'Who's *they*?'

She turned away to stare out of the window. After the first shock of his appearance her confidence was beginning to return.

'We've been looking all over for you,' Harry said. 'We want to ask you some questions about the murder of Peter Newton.'

'I didn't kill Peter,' she said angrily, turning round to meet his eyes. 'I didn't have anything to do with it.'

'We're not suggesting you did, but we still think you can help us by answering a few questions.'

'There's nothing I can tell you. I don't know anything about the murder.'

'There's a great deal you can tell us. We know, that you've been living with Newton. Haven't you been living with him for over, a month now?'

Judy answered coldly. 'I'm sorry. I can't help you.'

Harry leaned forward and tried to speak in a more friendly tone, to coax her into talking to him.

'Judy, listen. If you didn't kill Newton then the best thing you can do—'

'Don't call me Judy,' she whipped back. 'When I want you to call me Judy I'll say so.'

Harry sighed. He reached in his pocket for his cigarette case. The taxi had negotiated Trafalgar Square and was heading along the Mall.

'Where are you taking me?'

'To Scotland Yard. I want you to meet a friend of mine. Inspector Fletcher. He's in charge of ,the case.'

Judy gave an almost professional nod. 'I know Fletcher.' 'You know him?'

'I've seen him around. I'm glad he's a friend of *yours.*'

Harry surmised that this girl was a good deal less tough than she tried to make out. He moved over to the seat she was sitting on, letting the occasional seat snap back into place. He offered her his open cigarette case. She hesitated, then mink one. Before she had managed to get his lighter out, she had produced her own, lit the cigarette and replaced the lighter in the bag.

Harry lit his own cigarette.

'Do we have to go to Scotland Yard?' '

'Yes. I'm afraid we do.'

'Couldn't we go somewhere else?'

'Where – for instance?'

'For a moment he wondered whether she was going to try and buy him off, whether she was like those girls in Peter Newton's collection of photographs. But somehow she did not seem to fit into that category.

'I don't know. Anywhere we can talk.'

'I thought you didn't want to talk.'

'Not about Peter, I don't. But there are other things.'

'Such as?'

'Stop the damn cab and I'll tell you!'

Harry studied her face for a moment. She had attempted to run away from him once. This could be another device for trying to elude him. The floodlit shape of Buckingham Palace was looming up ahead. To the left were the dark lawns, pools and copses of St. James's Park. He made up his mind and leaned forward to pull aside the panel in the glass partition.

'Okay, driver. Pull up here, will you?'

The driver braked gently. He knew that a car was behind him, the same mini-van as he had held up in Charing Cross Road, and he did not want to be shunted from behind.

As he stopped and reached round to open the door for Judy he said: 'You happy about this, miss?'

'Yes.' Judy nodded. 'He's okay.'

Harry paid him off. He was keeping a close eye on Judy to make sure that she did not make a run for it, so he did not notice that the mini-van had quietly gone past and pulled in to the kerb fifty yards farther on.

As the cab drove away he steered Judy to a bench at the back of the broad footway, screened by a clump of bushes growing at the edge of the park.

'Now,' Harry prompted. 'What kind of things are we going to talk about – Miss Black?'

'Well, we could talk about – your father, for instance.'

They had reached the bench. From a dozen yards away a street lamp cast deep shadows through the branches that now hung over their heads. Judy sat down. She had thrown her cigarette away and was now reaching for another one.

'What do you know about my father?' Harry asked her very quietly. He felt a peculiar nervousness, a sense that he might be on the verge of some discovery that would destroy the image which he had built up of the father whom he had worshipped almost as a hero.

This time she accepted the light he offered her. She inhaled deeply and then breathed the smoke out slowly before she answered.

'I know who killed him.'

Chapter 2

The driver of the mini-van parked fifty yards farther on, leaned across and lowered the window on the passenger's side. He put his head out just far enough to see the couple settle themselves on the park bench and the flame of the lighter as they lit their cigarettes.

He slid back into the driver's seat. He had not stopped the engine. He engaged a gear and moved off towards Buckingham Palace. He was a small man with the hungry, lean look which some jockeys have. But Marty Smith was not a healthy specimen. His cheeks were pocked by the marks of acne and he had a facial twitch which caused his right lip, nostril and eye to flicker every few seconds. It was as if one half of his face was continually wincing as a result of a flat-handed slap.

He drove carefully round the Queen Victoria Memorial and came back down the Mall, now on the opposite side. A little way past the park bench where the couple still sat, he turned left, and parked the van facing the boundary at the back of Clarence House. It was not an authorised parking place but there were no coppers about. He climbed out, invisible under the shadows of the shrubs and trees and stared thoughtfully across the road. He would have given a lot to be able to hear what those two were saying.

'I met Peter about a year ago. I'm an actress, you know.' Judy smiled and then corrected herself. 'Well, a dancer, really. It was Peter who persuaded me to come down from Liverpool. He got me a part in that show at the St. Edward's theatre which was such a flop.'

'I gather he'd put quite a bit of money into it.'

'He had. But it didn't seem to worry him. He had plenty of the stuff and I must admit he was pretty generous with it. That's why in the end I accepted his invitation to move in with him.'

'Do you know where his money came from?'

'He told me he was in the property business. And he also had an uncle who died and left him a quarter of a million.'

'Hmm,' Harry sounded dubious. 'How did he treat you?'

Judy took out a fresh cigarette and lit it from the stub of the one she was smoking. 'We were very happy – at first anyway. Peter was really a very amusing person and good company. Then a funny thing happened—'

'Go on,' Harry prompted. Without much interest he was watching the small man who was dodging his way across the road. He disappeared down some path that led into St. James's Park. 'What sort of thing?'

'Well, we came back from a cocktail party the other night – it was the night before your father was killed. Peter was in a terrific mood. We were supposed to be going to Paris the next day. He said my education would not be complete until I'd been to Maxim's and the Tour d'Argent.'

'But you didn't go,' Harry prompted.

'No. It was very eerie. It must have been about ten when the door-bell rang and this man in evening dress came in. I was – well, I wanted to get some more clothes on so I skipped into the bedroom.'

'Did you see the man? Do you know who he was?'

'I recognised his voice straight away. His name is Arnold Conway. Peter. and I had been out once or twice with him and his wife Sybil. But he was talking to Peter in a way I'd never heard before. It made me frightened, but I couldn't help listening.'

'Can you remember what he said?'

Judy's brow puckered as she made the effort to remember. 'No, I can't really recall the words. Peter was obviously surprised to see Conway and asked him why he had come. And Conway told Peter that he had to be at Highgate Golf Club at ten o'clock sharp because that was the time Tom Dawson was going to be there. Peter made some sort of protest, but Arnold didn't give him a chance.'

She stopped, glancing nervously at Harry's face. 'Well, go on,' he said.

'There's nothing more. I walked out into the sitting-room then and Arnold suddenly became all affable. He left almost at once. Peter was obviously terribly upset but I was too. The idea of cancelling a trip to Paris for the sake of a game of golf . . .'

'That's what he told you?'

'Yes. He said he'd fixed up the game some time ago and had forgotten all about it. We ended up by having a proper row. I said something about him being Tam Owen's following dog and he went nearly berserk. Slapped me on the face and told me I must never mention that name – either to him or anyone else.'

'Tam Owen,' Harry repeated. 'Do you know anything about him?'

'Only that Peter used to be on the phone to him every day for about half an hour. I thought they were discussing property deals.'

In the telephone kiosk a hundred yards along the Mall, Marty Smith had just pushed in the coin which gave him his connection.

'Tam? Marty here . . . Look, he hasn't taken her to the Yard. Not yet. He stopped the taxi along the Mall . . . Sitting there talking, they are . . . But I thought you wanted her nicked.'

He put a finger in his free ear to mask the noise of a passing motor-scooter, his weasel face concentrated on what he was hearing.

'Linda said *what*? . . . Oh, suffering crows! . . . Yes, they're just down the road from me. You wani me to bring her back?' He listened for a moment. His twitch had started again. 'Okay, Tam. Okay, you're the boss.'

He hung up, left the booth, glanced all round him suspiciously, then set off along a path that led into the park. He did not follow it for long. He turned right, stepping over a barrier that was meant to keep people off the grass and slipped in amongst the shrubs which grew profusely at that part. The street lamp which he had noted near the park bench gave him a beacon to work towards.

He put a hand against his pocket to prevent the hard metal instrument which reposed there from bumping against his skinny hip.

'Well,' Judy was saying, 'the next day Peter went off to play golf. He came back earlier than I had expected. He looked awful, obviously very shaken, white as a sheet. He announced that he'd killed a man, just like that. I shall never forget the shock it gave me. Then he went on to make out that it had been an accident, that he'd gone out to practise and one of his shots had hit this man on the head.'

'I've heard that story, too,' Harry commented. 'Did you believe it?'

'Frankly, no. I could see he was lying. I asked him if he knew who the man was he'd killed and he told me Dawson. Well, I recognised the name at once as the one Arnold Conway had mentioned. But when I told Peter so he grabbed my arm so hard I've still got the bruises. He made me swear that I'd forget all about that conversation I'd overheard.'

Harry did not break the silence as she lit yet another cigarette and drew deeply on it. Her description had given him a vivid picture of what had happened in Peter Newton's flat. He could fill in the details for himself. No wonder the girl was frightened. If someone had found good reasons to murder Newton, doubtless to ensure his silence, there were just as good reasons to deal with Judy Black in the same way.

He cocked his head sideways. There was a rustling in the bushes behind them. Probably some small, timid animal which only dared to venture out of its hole at night.

'When I read about the accident,' Judy went on, resuming the narrative of her own accord, 'I was even more worried. I knew that Peter had not told the truth and I had a feeling, a horrible feeling, that your father's death was not an accident. Arnold Conway's words kept coming back to me.'

She was as nervy as a cat. Even the faint rustle of leaves in the thicket behind them made her turn her head fearfully.

'The next morning – yesterday, in fact, though it seems forever

– Peter received a phone call from Tam Owen. I was only half awake at the time and he took the call in the living-room. But I heard what he said.'

'What did you hear?' Harry had to prompt her.

Her voice had sunk very low. 'He said: "Tam, remember this! You're the one who killed Dawson. Not me. Now for God's sake leave me alone!" When he came back into the bedroom he was furious, almost trembling with rage. I kept my eyes shut and pretended to be asleep.'

'This man, Tam Owen. Were he and Peter in business together?'

'They may have been-but Owen was certainly the boss.' 'What makes you say that?'

'It was obvious. If Tam said "Go to Birmingham or Leeds or Manchester" Peter went. There was never any argument about it.'

'And Arnold Conway. How does he fit into the picture?' 'Arnold was a friend of Peter's. It was through him that he met Tam Owen.'

'Is that so?'

A couple of hundred yards away Harry could see the sentries on duty at Buckingham Palace being changed. A little party of three figures in scarlet tunics and busbies moved stiffly across the front of the floodlit building. The spectacle gave a sense of security and order to the whole scene.

'Now then, Miss Black. Tell me about—'

'Judy, please.' She made a brave attempt at a smile and put her hand on his arm. 'I'm sorry I was rude to you in the taxi. I didn't know who you were and I was frightened.'

Her smile and her touch had affected Harry more than he wanted to show. He tried to keep his tone on a dispassionate, official level, but a part of his mind could not help speculating on what it would be like to take this very attractive girl in his arms.

'Tell me about last night.'

'Peter took me out to dinner and we had another—' Her face puckered in distress.

'You had another row?'

'Yes. A terrible row this time. That's why I left him.'

'What time was this?'

'About ten o'clock.'

'Where did you leave him? In the restaurant?'

'No. We left the restaurant at about half-past nine and drove into Hyde Park. We sat in his car near the Serpentine for about half an hour.'

'And then what happened?'

'I told you,' Judy said, slightly uneasy under the questioning. 'I left him.'

'And what did you do?'

'I went for a walk.'

'Alone?'

'Yes. Of course.'

'Where did you walk?'

'In the park most of the time.'

'Did you talk to anyone – anyone you knew?'

She stared at him, aware now of the reason for these questions. The period they were speaking of was the time when Peter must have been murdered.

'No. No, I'm afraid I didn't.'

'Go on. What happened?'

'I – I stayed the night with a friend of mine. I wish to God I hadn't now. I wish I'd gone back to the flat. Perhaps if I'd done that – If only we hadn't had that bloody silly row.'

She was near to tears. Harry gave her a moment and then spoke in a more gentle tone.

'What was the row about, Judy?'

'Oh, it was nothing.'

'Was it about my father – about what happened?'

'No. It was the silliest thing.' She was fumbling in her handbag, this time for a handkerchief.

'What was it, Judy?'

'We had a row about the most ridiculous thing – a dog's collar.' She blew her nose and then gave a little laugh that was somehow more pathetic than tears. 'I told you it wasn't important.'

Harry swung round on the seat and gripped her by the shoulders. She gave a little cry at the sudden urgency in his manner and the strength of his grip.

'Judy, listen—'

He saw Judy's eyes suddenly widen and swing towards the bushes behind the seat. In the back of his mind he had heard the brush of a body against leaves, the crackle of a fallen branch breaking under a foot. Too late the sense of danger flooded over him. He began to rise and had half turned when Marty Smith's cosh caught him behind the ear.

He found himself falling into a gleaming whirlpool, its spinning sides reflecting Buckingham Palace, the dark trees of the park, Judy's mouth open in a silent scream, a pocked face contorted with hatred and violence . . .

'I'm all right, I tell you. I've got to get out of here. Now, will you please tell that idiot of a nurse to bring me my clothes!'

Harry had recovered consciousness to find himself in a bed in a hospital ward, surrounded by screens and naked except for a rather stiff kind of shift, not worthy of the name of nightgown. His protestations had cut no ice with the young and rather plain nurse who had been tucking the sheets in when he opened his eyes. Now, a somewhat formidable though not unattractive lady doctor had come to deal with this very difficult patient. She wore a white coat and the stethoscope dangled between her breasts.

'It is quite out of the question. You may have severe concussion and should remain in a darkened room for several days. Besides, we wish to X-ray your skull. It could be cracked.'

'It's not!' Harry said. 'Look, I've been laid out before. You don't know how thick a skull I've got.'

It was no good. The doctor was adamant. The best that Harry could do-was to persuade her to get a message through to Nat Fletcher at Scotland Yard, and he only achieved that by threatening to run naked down the corridor to the call box.

Nat was there in twenty minutes.

'So it was you!' was his first remark.

'It *is* me,' Harry corrected.

'No. I was referring to a report that came in just before we got your message. A passing motorist saw you being mugged on a bench in the Mall. He stopped and went back but all he found was you. The mugger and the girl who was with you had disappeared into St. James's Park. He decided that the first thing was to call an ambulance for you.'

'No sign of the girl?'

'No.' Nat sat down on the edge of the bed and lowered his voice. "He said she was a blonde girl. Not Judy Black by any chance?'

Harry nodded. Even that slight movement intensified the pain in his head. 'You've got to get me out of here, Nat. Those bitches have taken away my clothes—'

'All right.' Nat rose. 'Leave this to me.'

Harry never knew what story Nat told the doctor. She disassociated herself from the whole thing and did not appear again. A very disapproving nurse brought him his clothes and five minutes later he was climbing rather unsteadily into the passenger seat of the CID car which Nat was driving.

'It's very easy to criticise, Nat,' Harry said, as the car eased into the stream of traffic going round Hyde Park Corner. 'But what would you have done under the circumstances?'

'You know damn well what I would have done. I'd have taken her straight to Scotland Yard.'

'I wonder.'

'Harry, you've been an idiot. What the hell are we going to tell Yardley?'

'I'm not interested in Yardley.' Harry was stroking the back of his head where the lump raised by Marty's cosh was throbbing painfully. The moving traffic was not helping his feeling of nausea.

'Well, I am, and I'm investigating this case. You might try and remember that. When the Superintendent hears about this he'll go up like a flaming rocket.'

'Does he have to hear about it?'

For a moment Nat took his eyes off the traffic to glance at Harry.

'What have you got in mind?'

'If I can find Judy again. If I can find her before—'

'If – if – if,' Nat interrupted. 'Your only chance is another tip-off and you know it. You wouldn't have picked her up tonight if it hadn't been for that phone call. She knew the police were looking for her, so why the hell didn't she give herself up?'

'You know perfectly well why she didn't give herself up. She was frightened.'

'Frightened of what? If she didn't kill Newton what has she to be frightened of?'

The car was moving up Park Lane. There was some sort of big reception on at Grosvenor House and taxis were lining up at the entrance.

'Nat, for Pete's sake! This girl was living with Newton, she'd had a row with him and her alibi wasn't worth a cup of cold tea. Can you blame her for not going to the police?'

'Yes, well—' Nat was not going to let himself be influenced by what he regarded as Harry's sentimental attitude. 'I still say you should have brought her to the Yard, let her do her talking there.'

'All right, so I made a mistake.' Harry decided to concede the point. 'I made a mistake. It isn't the first one I've made and I don't suppose it'll be the last.'

Nat did not speak for a minute. He was closely watching the antics of a Jaguar driver who was continually swapping lanes.

'I'll tell you what I'll do, Harry,' he said, as Marble Arch loomed up ahead. 'I'll keep my mouth shut about tonight.'

'Thanks, chum.'

'I'll say nothing for forty-eight hours.' He gave concentration to getting round Marble Arch without being shunted by the drivers who were determined to force their way past every-thing else. 'But if you haven't found Judy Black by this time on Thursday, I'll tell Yardley what happened tonight. I shall have to.'

'Okay,' Harry said with satisfaction. 'Now you tell me something and be honest about it. Do you believe Judy Black's story? Do you believe what she told me?'

'I believe part of it. I believe she was telling the truth about your father – about what happened the night before he was killed. But I don't think she was telling the truth about Newton.'

'Why do you say that?'

'Because he wasn't in the property racket at all. He was in a very different game. Judy told you he was working for that man – what's his name again?'

'Owen. Tam Owen.'

Nat nodded confirmation. 'The property business is just a cover. Owen runs a call-girl set-up, if you ask me. But it's a very special service he gives, very special girls for very special people – high executives, V.I.P.s, big businessmen visiting London. And I don't have to tell you what the possibilities of that line of business are.'

'So you think Judy knew this?'

'Of course she knew of it,' Nat said scornfully. 'She must have done.'

Harry shook his head, carefully but obstinately. 'I'm sorry, Nat. But I don't agree with you.'

'No, I didn't think you would somehow,' Nat said. His voice was heavy with sarcasm as he added: 'Read any good romantic novels lately?'

'Oh, I know what you're thinking,' Harry said, an unwonted hostility in his tone. 'I know what's 'at the back of that sordid old mind of yours. But you're mistaken.'

'Then that makes two of us,' Nat commented drily, swinging the car into Gloucester Place.

The rest of the trip to the shop in the Finchley Road was completed in a rather taut silence.

Nat had drawn up at the kerb and Harry had opened the door when the former reached into the back of the car for a brief-case. He opened it and took out the much discussed dog collar.

'Here's the collar, by the way. We've finished with it.' 'Have the labs seen it?'

'They've seen it all right. It's been through the whole building. The report's negative. It's just a perfectly ordinary dog collar. What the devil Newton meant by that note of his I can't imagine.'

Harry was standing on the pavement. He bent down to take the collar from Nat. 'No, neither can I.'

'What was it he said? "This is why your father was killed"?' 'Yes. I think those were the words.' Harry closed the door. 'Good night, Nat. And thanks.'

'You're sure you're okay now?'

'Yes. I'll be all right.'

'Remember what the doctor said. No more hi-jinks and early bed.'

Harry watched the car drive away. He still felt a little unsteady on his feet. When he went to the street door leading to the flat he saw that in his haste to reach Judy Black he had left it unlocked.

Though he was sure he had not switched on the lights over the stairway to the flat, he saw that they were burning now. His experience in St. James's Park had made him wary. He certainly did not relish the thought of another crack on the skull. So it was slowly and cautiously that he moved up the stairs to the landing outside his flat.

The figure standing with his back to him could hardly have been more reassuring. He was wearing a dark-grey pin-striped business suit. The stiff white collar emerged a good half-inch from the top of the jacket. On his head he wore a bowler hat and a tightly rolled umbrella dangled from his left forearm. With his right index finger he was impatiently pressing the bell push.

More than anything he looked like someone who had come to sell insurance or managed bonds.

'Can I help you?' Harry said.

The figure spun round, blinking with surprise. The face was moon-shaped, rather pallid and apologetic, the skin pink and smooth as if only recently shaved.

'Oh – er.' The man was trying to recover from the fright Harry had given him. 'I was looking for a Mr. Harry Dawson.' 'Well, that's me.'

'Ah.' The tall man nodded eagerly. 'I'm so sorry dropping in on you unannounced like this.'

'Well, who are you?' Harry was making no move to open the door. 'What do you want?'

'Oh, I do beg your pardon. I'm Mrs. Rogers' nephew, Hubert Rogers. We haven't actually met before but I'm sure we've heard a great deal about each other from my aunt.'

'Yes, of course!' Harry tried to conceal his surprise. He had never pictured Hubert as being like this. He was the member of the family who had come up in the world, got himself a job with a big insurance company. His neat suit and carefully knotted tie sat uneasily on him as if he had not yet adjusted himself to his respectability.

'I'm sorry, Mr. Rogers. Do come in, please.'

Harry turned his key in the door and held it back for Hubert Rogers to enter. He followed him into the sitting-room, switching on lights as he went. Hubert put his bowler and umbrella carefully down on the table in the middle of the room.

'Can I get you a drink?'

Hubert gave his thin smile. 'That's most kind of you, but – I'm afraid I don't drink.'

Harry reached for the cigarette box. 'A cigarette, then?'

Hubert's smile became even more apologetic. 'I'm afraid I don't smoke either. No vices, Mr. Dawson – except one, perhaps.' He fixed Harry with his pale, unemotional eyes. 'I have a disturbing habit of coming straight to the point, at least, so my colleagues tell me.'

'I wouldn't have said that was necessarily a vice, Mr. Rogers. In my job we'd consider it a virtue.'

Hubert gave a small, dry laugh. 'Yes. Yes, I suppose you would.'

He ran a finger round inside of his starched collar to ease the pressure of the front stud on his Adam's apple.

'Mr. Dawson, I'm worried about my aunt, quite perturbed about her in fact. That's why I decided to have a word with you about it.'

He had an accent which did not quite ring true. His way of speaking had been carefully adjusted to match his style of dress but an occasional mispronounced word still managed to get through.

'What are you disturbed about? Incidentally, you know, of course, that your aunt is not with me any longer.'

'Yes. I understand she's working at that new hotel, the Plaza something or other. Plaza Royal, I think it is.'

'That's right.' Harry realised that he was not going to get rid of Hubert very quickly. His head was throbbing abominably and he wondered whether he was visibly swaying on his feet. But he knew that he must make the effort to keep going a little longer. He was curious to find out what had brought Mrs. Rogers' nephew to the flat at this late hour.

Hubert gladly accepted the invitation to sit down.

'I'm very fond of my aunt and I owe her a great deal, he said in his precise way. 'It was she who looked after me when my parents died. But just now I'm very worried about her. I think she's – well, not to put too fine a point upon it, I think she's going round the bend.'

Hubert emphasised the slang expression as if it was very daring of him to use it.

'Why do you say that?'

'Well – it's very extraordinary. She's telephoned me the Lord knows how many times and she's always on about the same thing. She keeps saying – this is quite absurd and I do apologise for repeating it – that you've stolen something of hers.'

'Stolen something? Good Lord, what am I supposed to have stolen?'

Again Hubert gave his diffident little laugh. 'That's just it. It's quite absurd. She says you've stolen a dog collar.'

Harry studied him for a few moments. A dog collar was the last thing he had heard mentioned before he was knocked unconscious. Automatically he ran a hand over the subsiding bump.

'I presume she means the collar my father gave her for Zero?'

'Yes. That's right. Why she keeps on about it, I don't know. Still, she was very fond of your father. But now that she has the dog back she should be grateful. In any case, she can well afford to buy another collar for the wretched animal. In fact, I've even offered to buy her one myself—'

'Yes, but it isn't another collar she wants, Mr. Rogers.' Harry had put his hand into his jacket pocket. 'It's this one.'

Hubert blinked with surprise as Harry produced the collar. He stood up and came over to his side.

'Is this the collar she's making all the fuss about?'

'Yes.'

'Good heavens !' Hubert held out his hand. 'May I?'

'Yes, of course.'

Harry watched him as he turned the collar over and over several times in his hand before returning it.

'It's a very nice one, very nice, but I fail to see what all the excitement's about.'

'So do I, Mr. Rogers.' Harry stood up and went to put the collar down on the desk. 'Anyway, you can tell your aunt if she gets in touch with me she can have it back.'

'Really?' Hubert seemed delighted that his visit had been so fruitful. He picked his hat and umbrella off the table. 'Oh, well, that solves the problem. Thank you, Mr. Dawson, I'm very grateful to you.'

Relieved that the interview had been so short and simple, Harry was shepherding his guest towards the door.

As he crossed the hall, Hubert paused and turned.

'It's really none of my business and I hope you don't mind my asking but – why didn't you give my aunt the collar the other day when she picked up the poodle?'

'For the simple reason that I hadn't got it. Superintendent Yardley had it.'

Hubert's eyes were beady with curiosity, but Harry merely shrugged.

'He was taking a look at it, Mr. Rogers. But I told your aunt all this. She knew Scotland Yard had the collar.'

'Really? Well, there you are, you see? She never told me that. Never said a blessed word about it.'

Hubert shook his head hopelessly and held out his hand to Harry. It was a limp hand, rather sweaty on the palm. 'Thank you, Mr. Dawson,' he said again.

Harry held the front door open for him. 'Ask Mrs. Rogers to give me a ring.'

'Yes. I'll certainly do that. And again, many thanks. Good night.'

'Good night.'

Harry waited only as long as politeness demanded before closing the door. Instead of going back to the sitting-room he went into his own bedroom which opened off the hall. It was a small room but the use of ship's furniture bought when a famous liner had gone to the breakers gave it a compact, masculine look. Harry opened the cabinet above the wash-basin, took four aspirins from a bottle and washed them down with a glass of water. A glance in the mirror gave him a shock. The face was that of a man ten years older.

Tonight, somehow, he'd have to catch up on his sleep.

He was going through the sitting-room to the kitchen when the collar lying on the desk caught his eye. He paused, then picked it up and walked into the box-room, whence the spiral staircase led down into the office.

Below, the lights which burned all night gave him enough illumination to descend the spiral staircase and find the safe, camouflaged behind a dummy fireplace. He had to use the mnemonic rhyme his father had taught him before he could remember the combination. When the door swung open he placed the collar on a shelf inside and made sure the safe was firmly locked on it.

The call came through about two hours after the shop had opened next morning. Harry had been dealing with a few problems which Douglas Croft had not been able to solve for himself. A long night's sleep had enabled him to recover from the blow on his head. He had gone out to have a word with Liz at the front of the shop when the telephone rang in the .office. A moment later Douglas put his head round the glass-panelled door.

'It's for you, Mr. Dawson. Mrs. Rogers wants to speak to you.'

Harry hurried towards the office and waited till Douglas had closed the door, leaving him alone, before he spoke into the receiver.

'Mrs. Rogers?'

'Hallo, Mr. Dawson. I'm sorry to bother you, but I've just been talking to Hubert, my nephew. He tells me he saw you last night.'

74

Harry could tell by her voice that she was nervous and embarrassed. He thought he could hear the sound of traffic faintly in the background and guessed that she was in a public call box.

'He did, Mrs. Rogers. We had quite an interesting little chat.'

' – understand you've got the collar back – Zero's collar?'

'Yes, I have,' Harry said reassuringly. 'Would you like it?'

'Yes, I would, Mr. Dawson,' she said quickly, obviously relieved at his suggestion. 'Thank you very much. Would you be kind enough to post it to me? My address is—'

'No, I'm sorry, Mrs. Rogers. I'd rather not post it. As a matter of fact I want something from you too. Call it a swop if you like.'

Harry absent-mindedly shifted a book which was in danger of being knocked to the floor. It was an *A.A. Members Handbook*, open at the section listing towns in alphabetical order.

'What is it you want?' Mrs. Rogers' voice was nervous again after the short pause.

'Information.'

'About what?'

'About a friend of yours – Tam Owen.'

After the briefest hesitation she came back very sharply, almost angrily. 'I don't know anyone called Tam Owen.'

'I think you do, Mrs. Rogers. The collar's here if you want it. Drop in at the flat any time.'

'No, wait a minute!' There was panic in her voice as she sensed that he was about to ring off. 'I don't want to come to your flat. It's not – it's not convenient. I – Do you know a pub called the Golden Plough?'

'In St. John's Wood?'

'Yes. Meet me there this evening, Mr. Dawson. About seven. In the saloon bar. I'll be there.'

She had rung off. Harry put the receiver down slowly. His eye rested on the open A.A. book he had rescued from falling. It was open at the As and someone had put a cross against the name of a town.

Aldeburgh.

*

The Golden Plough was a modern inn with several bars and a small restaurant. The saloon bar was very modern – mirrors, concealed lighting and leatherette. At one end of the horseshoe-shaped bar was a snack counter with a dozen high stools lined up before glass cases containing cold joints, pork pies and salads. Tape-recorded music floated discreetly out over the hum of conversation, like oil over troubled waters.

When Harry entered there were already a number of people sitting at tables lining the edge of the room. Two men were embarking on plates of food at the snack counter. Another, older man was hovering near the bar, glancing hopefully towards the door leading to the Ladies' Powder Room. He was wearing a fawn coat with a velvet collar and a broad brimmed round, reddening a little either with surprise or embarrassment. It seemed that he had dressed with particular care as if for some special occasion.

'How are you?' Harry said, as they shook hands.

'I'm very well, thank you, sir. I haven't seen you here before. Is this one of your usual haunts?'

'No. I'm afraid it isn't. I'm meeting a friend. Is this your local?'

'Yes, my shop's just round the corner. Oh!'

The little exclamation was caused by the appearance of a red-headed woman who had just come out of the ladies' room. She was aged about thirty, with a strongly defined figure but rather hard features. When she saw Harry talking to Heaton she checked, then made up her mind to brazen it out. She walked towards the two men, smiling slightly.

'I'm ready, duckie,' she told Heaton, to his slight embarrassment. 'Has Chow been behaving himself?'

'Yes. He's been as good as gold.'

She took the cat and perched it on her own shoulder. 'No tiddles, eh? Good boy.'

Knowing that Harry was looking at her she directed her bold, professional stare right at him and smiled challengingly.

'Excuse me,' Harry said. 'Aren't you a friend of Judy Black's?'

'Oh, forgive me,' Heaton butted in. 'I should have introduced you. This is Miss Linda Wade. Mr. Dawson – of Scotland Yard.'

Linda was still meeting Harry's eye. Her smile had not altered.

'Pleased to meet you. Did you say Judy Black? No. I don't know anyone of that name.'

'But surely you were with her last night – at a restaurant called Chez Maurice in Greek Street'

'No. I've just told you,' Linda said amicably, 'I don't know anyone of that name. Sorry.' She turned and hooked her arm possessively through Heaton's. 'Come on, duckie. I'm getting hungry.'

Heaton gave a smile which was half apologetic and half proud. His discomfiture at being surprised at his trysting place was superseded by the knowledge that the eyes of every man in the room were covertly watching Linda's hip movement as she steered him out of the bar.

Harry watched them go, then moved across to the bar. The velvet-jacketed barman moved swiftly to serve him.

'A scotch and soda, please.'

'Excuse me, sir. I couldn't help hearing your name mentioned. It's Mr. Dawson, isn't it?'

'Yes.'

'There's been a phone message for you, sir, from a Mrs. Rogers. She's very sorry. She won't be able to keep the appointment.'

Harry bit back an exclamation of annoyance. 'When was this? When did she phone?'

'Oh, about half an hour ago.'

'She didn't say anything else?'

'Yes. She said she'd phone you later tonight, sir. At your flat.'

'I see. Thank you.'

'Scotch and soda, you said, sir?'

'Make it a double. No ice.'

The phone was ringing inside the flat as Harry inserted his key in the door to the hall. He opened it quickly, burst through the hall and scooped up the receiver.

'Hallo?' No answer. 'Hallo. Mrs. Rogers?'

There was still no reply. Harry tapped the receiver with his finger-nails. Instantly the dialling tone began.

'Oh, damn!'

Harry slammed the receiver down and stood staring balefully at it. After a moment it started ringing again. He let it go on for about ten seconds, then picked it up. Once again the dialling tone recommenced.

Fuming with annoyance he peeled off his overcoat and flung it across the settee. He took a cigarette from the box and lit it, half expecting the phone to ring again.

When it didn't he went out into the hall and pushed open the door of his own room, snapping on the light as he did so. He took off his jacket, opened the wardrobe door and reached for a coat hanger.

The door swung open, the mirror fixed on the inside panning across the room like a cine-camera. It reached the bed, swung past it.

Suddenly Harry grabbed the door, moved it back through twenty degrees. Reflected on its surface was a sight which he could not believe was real. Sprawled across his bed a bulky woman's body lay face downwards. The hat with the plastic flowers had been knocked askew and her skirt had ridden up above her podgy knees. The ivory handle of a kitchen carving-knife stuck out from below her ribs.

Harry had experienced this feeling before. It had been when he was in Yardley's office at Scotland Yard. Now the sense of unreality made him wonder if he was dreaming. Here he was, sitting in his own flat, being questioned by his own Chief Superintendent. What was frightening was that, although he had all along stuck rigidly to the truth, his answers sounded so lame and false.

'If you don't believe me, if you don't believe a word I say, there seems to be very little point in my saying anything.'

He stood up to collect another cigarette from the box, his third since the police had arrived. Normally he was a very moderate smoker.

'Now, wait a minute. Let's get this straight.' Yardley was watching him as he lit the cigarette, no doubt to see whether his hands were trembling. 'I'm not disputing the fact that you went to this pub. In any case your story can be checked with the barman and this other man – Heaton, I think you said his name was. But what I don't understand is why you had to go all the way up to the Golden Plough.'

'But I've told you why I went there,' Harry said with exasperated emphasis. 'To meet Mrs. Rogers.'

From where he was standing now he could see through into his own bedroom. It was thronged with members of the Murder Squad, all purposefully going through the routine with which Harry was all too familiar.

'But why didn't she come here to the flat?' Yardley was checking over the notes he had made in his book. 'What was the point of meeting in a pub in St. John's Wood?'

'I don't know. The pub was her idea, sir. Not mine.'

He turned his back on Yardley and walked over to the mantelpiece. In the centre of it stood a clock in a silver case with an inscription on the base. It was a tribute to his father from some boys' organisation he had done a lot for. The world seemed to have gone mad since that morning Tom Dawson had set off for the Westgate Golf Club.

'You asked her to come here and she refused.' Yardley's tone was ominously soothing. 'So you arranged to meet her in the saloon bar at the Golden Plough. That's your story, Dawson?'

Harry swung round. He would have met Yardley's eye if the big man had been looking at him. But the Superintendent was closing his book and putting it in his pocket.

'That's what happened, sir. It's not just my story.'

The hostile silence was broken by the appearance of Nat Fletcher in the doorway. His face wore a closed, unemotional expression which Harry could understand. The police officer who has to come to the scene of the murder, examine the corpse, watch the police doctor, the pathologist, the forensic expert going about their macabre duties has to detach himself emotionally from what he sees.

'We've finished, sir. We've got everything we want.'

Yardley grunted and began to heave himself forward in the deep armchair. 'Right.'

Nat turned to Harry, still with that strange, remote expression. 'You're certain, absolutely certain that you did not touch the body?'

Harry shook his head. 'I did not touch anything. I did not even go near the bed.'

'Good. Now, what about next of kin? Is there a Mr. Rogers?'

'No. He died about ten years ago. She had no family; but there's a nephew – Hubert Rogers. He works for the Storm Insurance Company.'

'In London?'

'Yes. I think so.'

Yardley had finally got his weight on to his feet. 'All right, leave that to me, Nat.'

His eye caught the clock on the mantelpiece. 'Good heavens! We've been here nearly two hours ! I'll see you in the morning, Nat.'

'Yes, sir.'

Yardley gave Harry a curt nod and walked ponderously out into the hall. Nat crossed to the chair on which he had left his outdoor coat.

'He doesn't believe me, Nat,' Harry said. 'He just doesn't believe a single word I say.'

Nat slowly put his coat on, checked that he had not left anything else in the room and only then did he look at Harry. His expression was puzzled and there was something there which Harry could not define. It was not exactly hostility or suspicion, but the old warmth, the old friendliness was gone.

'I'll be seeing you, Harry,' he said and followed his superior out of the flat.

Harry stayed in the sitting-room, smoking far more cigarettes than he really wanted, sipping at the coffee he had made for himself. He could hear the police and their assistants still working away in his bedroom, but he did not go through to see how they were getting on. These men were his colleagues and yet they were now on the other side of some invisible barrier. He was beginning to understand how a sane man might feel if he were certified for forced sequestration in a mental home.

They seemed to take an unconscionable time getting finished with the job. It was midnight before the ambulance came to take away the mortal remains of Mrs. Rogers. Twenty minutes later the outer door slammed and he knew that he was alone in the flat.

He had already decided to sleep in his father's room rather than his own. Everything he would need was still there, shaving things, clean pyjamas, a made-up bed. Even the individual smell of his father still pervaded the room. Harry pulled the curtains aside and stared up at the night sky.

The sound of the door-bell broke into his long reverie. He pulled the curtains back and with a sense of mounting resentent went to open the door. The time was twenty minutes to one. Probably one of those stolid detective sergeants had forgotten something.

But the person who stood on his doormat was no dour police-man. It was Hubert Rogers; but a very different Hubert Rogers from the prim and correct gentleman who had called the day before. He had all the appearance of a man who has been hauled out of bed just as his beauty-sleep was beginning. His hair was hastily combed. He had pulled on a pair of old-fashioned grey flannel trousers and a green polo-necked sweater. His feet had been pushed into a pair of North African moccasins, probably purchased in a wild moment on some package tour.

'Mr. Rogers,' Harry said unnecessarily. Of course, he should have guessed that Hubert's first reaction on hearing the news would be to rush round here. 'You'd better come in.'

'Dawson, is this true – about my aunt? Is it really true?'

'Yes. I'm afraid it is.'

Hubert came into the hall, glancing fearfully towards the now locked and sealed door of Harry's bedroom.

'My God, I just can't believe it A man called Yardley – he must be the Superintendent Yardley you mentioned – came to see me. A big heavy chap.'

'Yes. That's him.' Harry closed the door of the flat.

'I was in bed. I make a point of having one early night a week and—'

He broke off and to Harry's astonishment seized him by the arm. 'Dawson, what happened? What on earth happened?'

'Come on into the living-room. Let me get you a drink. You look as if you could use one.'

He put his hand on the dishevelled man's shoulder to shepherd him past the murder room and into the living-room.

'Now, what'll it be? Whisky—'

'I don't drink,' Hubert said doggedly. 'Please tell me what happened.'

'Didn't the Superintendent tell you?'

Harry had decided that even if Hubert Rogers was refusing a drink he was going to have one himself. He poured it at the cocktail cabinet while Hubert repeated what he had heard from Yardley.

'Yes, that's true. That's exactly what happened.'

'But I just don't understand this.' Hubert was staring at him with an expression in which there was both alarm and accusation. 'When I spoke to my aunt—'

'Rogers, please sit down,' Harry cut in crisply. 'There's something I want to say to you.'

Hubert looked round him and then decided on one of the upright chairs. Harry settled himself more comfortably in the chair Yardley had used.

'I won't deny that your aunt and I never really hit it off together. Frankly, I was not sorry when she decided to leave me. I never really liked her and I don't think she liked me either. But I didn't kill her, Rogers.'

'Good God, I never thought you did,' Hubert protested, moving uneasily on the chair. 'Such a thing never entered my head. And you're absolutely wrong when you say my aunt didn't like you. She was very fond of you, Dawson – fond of both you and your father.'

Hubert stood up and paced across the room, perhaps to get out of the line of Harry's sceptical gaze.

82

'But there's something I don't understand about tonight. Something that just doesn't add up.'

'What do you mean?' Harry prompted.

'After I saw you I telephone my aunt and told her you'd got Zero's collar back and that you were prepared to return it to her. She was delighted.'

'Go on.'

'This afternoon she dropped in on me unexpectedly. She said she had spoken to you on the phone, you'd been charming to her and that she was coming round here this evening to see you.'

Harry stood up in such surprise that he knocked his glass of whisky from the arm of the chair. It shattered on the carpet, spreading a small stain on the pile. He made no move to retrieve it.

'She said she was coming here, to the flat?'

'Yes. She said you had asked her round for a drink, some time this evening. The poor dear was really quite flattered.'

'But – but this isn't true!'

There was obstinacy in the pale eyes that met Harry's 'That's what she told me, Dawson.'

Harry fought to hold down a rising sense of despair. 'Did – did you tell the Superintendent this?'

'Yes. Of course I did, my dear fellow. What else could I tell him?'

Next morning Harry found it hard to concentrate on any thing for long. It might have helped to go out but he knew that sooner or later Yardley would turn up again and he wanted to get it over with. In the end he was glad that he had stayed in. It had resulted in him having a very interesting talk with Douglas Croft. He was still in the office at the back of the shop when he saw the police car draw up outside. Yardley swung his legs out and then used the top of the open door to haul himself upright. The slim and lithe figure of Nat had emerged from the opposite side.

Harry turned to Liz. 'Go and tell them I'm in here, Liz, will you?'

Liz went running towards the street while Douglas Croft

gathered up the samples he had been discussing with Harry. He was in a hurry to make himself scarce. Nat Fletcher had caught him before he left home that morning and subjected him to a series of quick-fire questions. He'd wound up feeling that he had been tied in knots.

'May I sit down?' was Yardley's first remark as he came into the small office. 'My feet are killing me this morning. You always hear these corny jokes about policemen and their feet, but, by God, they're true!'

He sat down in the metal-framed office chair Harry pulled forward. Nat remained standing, leaning one elbow on the top of a filing-cabinet.

Yardley went straight to the point. 'I saw Mr. Rogers last night – the nephew.'

'Yes. I know.'

'Then you know about his aunt calling in yesterday afternoon and what she said to him?'

'Yes.' Harry felt that the blood was draining from his face. He knew his voice was strained. 'It's not true, sir.'

Yardley looked at him with his head on one side and then shot a look at Nat. Nat took the cue to come in on the questioning.

'You mean, you don't believe Rogers? You don't believe his aunt did call and tell him—'

'Yes, I think she did tell him that she was coming here but she was not telling the truth.'

Yardley asked: 'Why would she tell a lie about a thing like that?'

'I don't know, sir. I wish I did. But she did lie and we've got proof of it.'

'What sort of proof, Harry?' The question came from Nat.

'She telephoned the pub, and left a message for me. Why should she do that if we'd arranged to meet here in the first place?'

'*Someone* telephoned the pub,' Yardley corrected him. 'We don't know for certain it was Mrs. Rogers.'

The telephone on the desk at which Harry was sitting started to ring.

'The barman didn't know her,' Nat agreed. 'It was just a voice on the phone, so far as he was concerned.'

'Yes, I know, Nat, but if you're going to doubt every—' Harry broke off in annoyance. It was impossible to talk against the insistence of the bell, which had been set so that it was audible at the front of the shop. He picked up the receiver.

'Hallo? . . . Yes, speaking ... Yes, he's here. He's just arrived.'

He handed the instrument to Nat. 'It's your office.'

To his surprise Nat did not take the phone.

'Is there anywhere else I can take the call?'

'Yes, if you go up those stairs and through the box-room you'll find yourself in the living-room. I can switch the call through to you there.'

He waited till Nat had clattered up the fire-escape, crossed the room above and picked up the phone. Then he put his own instrument down. The fact that Nat had not wanted to take the call in his presence emphasised brutally the rift which had opened up between him and the two police officers. He was not a colleague now; he was a suspect in a double murder case.

He turned back to Yardley, waiting for the questions he knew would come. He must keep his head, stick to his story. In the end something would happen which would show that he was not lying.

'Dawson, I think if I remember rightly you told me that Mrs. Rogers was *working* at the Royal Plaza.'

'Yes. That's what I said.'

Yardley shook his head, as if he was genuinely sorry to demolish yet another of Harry's allegations. 'She was staying there, as a guest. She had a room on the tenth floor. She'd booked it for five weeks. It was costing her twelve pounds a day – without meals.'

'But how on earth could Mrs. Rogers afford to pay that sort of money?'

'I don't know.'

It took Harry a moment to readjust to this extraordinary revelation. 'Does her nephew know about this?'

'He does now. Nat told him this morning.'

'What did he say?'

'He was puzzled. Very puzzled. Like you he was under the impression his aunt was working at the hotel.'

'I don't understand this,' Harry said with feeling. 'I'm damned if I do.'

'Neither do I. But then there's lots of things I don't understand.' Yardley stood up, looming over Harry, his bulk seeming to fill the little office. But when he spoke his voice was quiet. 'I wish to God you'd put me in the picture, Dawson.'

'Me?' The accusation implied in the remark shook Harry so much that he answered like a small boy caught in the act by his school teacher.

'Yes, you.' Yardley's frown had deepened. 'In my opinion you're holding out on me. You haven't told me the truth. You've made false statements about almost everything.'

'I told you the truth about the Conways, and what happened? You didn't believe me.'

'How could I believe you when the Conways both denied the story and your cheque was found on Newton? And all that damn nonsense about Arnold Conway and a wheelchair. When I spoke to Inspector Emerson about it he laughed himself silly.'

'Nevertheless, it was the truth. And I'll tell you something else about the Conways. Something you won't believe.'

'Go on,' Yardley urged him. But Harry still hesitated. It went against the grain to reveal something that would tarnish the image of Tom Dawson.

He could see through to the front of the shop where the attractive outline of Liz Mason's athletic body was silhouetted against the light from the street beyond. That made him think about Judy Black. Two nights and a day had passed since he had seen her and there was still no clue as to where she might be hiding. He had spent the whole of the previous afternoon quartering the Soho area, hoping he might have the luck to catch a glimpse of her.

Yardley was still looking down at him, waiting for him to finish his statement.

'She was having an affair with my father,' he said quietly.

'Mrs. Conway, you mean?'

'Yes.'

'Who told you this?'

Harry nodded towards the shop where the fair-headed Douglas in his dashing sports jacket was chatting up a customer. 'Doug. Douglas Croft. He went down to Worthing one weekend. Sybil Conway and my father were staying at the same hotel.'

Yardley gave a low whistle, whether of envy or disapproval it was hard to say.

'Why didn't you mention this before?'

'He only told me about it this morning, shortly before you arrived.'

'Is he sure about it?'

'Yes. There's no doubt about it. At first my father pretended not to recognise Douglas but then he came clean. He told Doug that Mrs. Conway was married to a permanent invalid who could only get about in a wheelchair, and so there never could be any question of a divorce. He asked Douglas to say nothing about it.'

'How did Croft know her name was Conway? I'm surprised at your father mentioning her name.'

'He didn't. But she phoned Douglas the other day about a pearl necklace my father was supposed to be having repaired for her. She didn't know what had happened to it and she thought perhaps the receipt was in the office and Douglas could get it for her. She wanted him to send it to her at some hotel in Aldeburgh.'

'Was it in the office?'

'No. It wasn't.'

'And you think Mrs. Rogers knew about this – your father and Mrs. Conway?'

'Yes,' Harry said unhappily. 'I do.'

Yardley stared out thoughtfully into the shop, where Douglas was extolling the virtues of a new brand of squash racquet to a dubious young man.

The feet of Nat Fletcher clattered on the spiral staircase. Yardley looked at him enquiringly, wondering whether the message was something that could be mentioned in the presence of Dawson.

'There's been a message for you from Hampstead, sir. From Inspector Emerson.'

'Dick Emerson? What does he want?'

'Well, I got the message second-hand, but I gather he wants to talk to you fairly urgently.' Nat glanced towards Harry. 'Something about a wheelchair.'

Yardley had no difficulty in recognising the Bentley which was pulling out of the forecourt of Hampstead Police Station as he drove in. Conway was driving and his wife was beside him. They looked tired and bad-tempered and far too involved in some personal squabble to notice the inconspicuous CID car.

Emerson was an old friend of Yardley's. They spent some time on reminiscences before the Inspector got down to the business in hand.

'The Conway residence was burgled somewhere around midnight last night. Fortunately one of our patrols noticed something so we were on to it pretty quickly. The place had been absolutely ransacked, but we couldn't tell whether anything was missing till the Conways came back. They were pretty furious at being hauled out of their beds in Aldeburgh at one a.m. They got back here about four.'

Yardley sipped at the cup of tea which one of Emerson's girl clerks had brought.

'Now, Hal, this is the curious part and this is why I sent for you. When I first went over to the house I saw something in one of, the bedrooms which – in view of our recent conversation – immediately aroused my interest. I don't have to tell you what it was.'

'A wheelchair,' Yardley said, like someone offering an answer to a child's crossword puzzle.

'Right. The chair was in a cupboard, a sort of built-in wardrobe, the door of which had been forced open.'

Emerson, an inveterate pipe smoker, took up his pipe and began to fill it from the pouch that lay on his desk.

'When the Conways got back, I asked them to take a good

look round the house so that we could list the items stolen. They said that as far as they could tell nothing had been taken. It seemed incredible, so I asked Conway to make a tour of the house with me. I made a point of investigating the cupboard with him. The chair wasn't there. It had gone.'

'Just like that?'

'Yes. It had disappeared. Obviously someone had taken it away, *after* I had seen it.'

'Did you make any comment?'

'No. I drew Conway's attention to the forced lock and asked him to make sure that nothing had been taken. He said: 'No, Inspector, everything's just the same. Nothing's been taken.' Those were his exact words.'

Yardley breathed a long sigh of relief. For some reason the chair he was sitting in had become more comfortable. 'Thank you, Dick. By the way, I saw the Conways driving away just as I arrived. They didn't seem to be in the best of moods.'

Emerson put down the match with which he had lit his pipe. Coils of blue-grey smoke swirled up through the sun-light shafting from the window.

'Yes. That brings me to the next thing. There's a new, development. The Conways came in to see me about half an hour ago. Mrs. Conway said she had now discovered that a pearl necklace had been stolen. She gave me the description of it. I must admit it seemed a little odd that an intruder should break into a house full of valuable objects and just pinch a pearl necklace.'

'Did she say how much the necklace was worth?'

'Yes, about five hundred pounds.' Emerson placed his box of matches over the bowl of his pipe to make it draw better. 'But it's that business about the wheelchair that puzzles me.'

'You're not the only one, Dick.'

At about the same time as Yardley drove in to the police station at Hampstead, Harry was opening the door of Sidney Heaton's pet shop. Heaton was serving a customer but he gave Harry a friendly nod.

When his customer had departed, laden with an assortment of pet foods, Heaton walked down the shop to where Harry was standing.

'Good morning, Mr. Dawson. I was expecting you. I thought you'd be dropping in on me some time this morning.'

'I take it you've already seen a colleague of mine?'

'Yes. Superintendent Yardley, I think he said his name was. He called very early, before I was open, in fact. He wanted to know if I'd seen you last night. What's it all about, Mr. Dawson? He was frightfully evasive.'

The cage which had contained the marmoset monkey was empty now. Somebody must have bought it. Harry hoped the little animal had gone to a good home.

He said: 'Mrs. Rogers, my housekeeper – or rather my ex-housekeeper – was found murdered last night.'

Sidney Heaton's hand went to his mouth. Harry had not intended to shock him so profoundly with the brutal announcement.

'Murdered?' Heaton had difficulty in finding his voice. 'Good God! Where? Where did it happen?'

'In my flat . . .' Harry began. He was watching Heaton's reactions with detached interest.

'But what an appalling thing ! Have you any idea who . . .'

'Mr. Heaton, forgive me,' Harry cut in. 'I'm in rather a hurry this morning, and I've one or two questions I'd like to ask you.'

'By all means.' Heaton tried to get a grip on himself. He looked up at Harry with an obedient expression. 'Anything I can do to help you, Mr. Dawson.'

'Then, would you mind telling me who that girl was, the girl I saw you with last night? I think you introduced her as Linda Wade.'

'Oh, dear.' Heaton dropped his eyes. His cheeks reddened with embarrassment but a slightly roguish expression had crept into his eyes. 'I wish you hadn't asked that question.'

'Is she a friend of yours?'

'Good gracious no! I assure you most of my friends are . . . I really don't know anything about her.'

Harry put on his most formal expression. 'Mr. Heaton, I'm investigating a murder case. I want you to tell me all you know about Linda Wade.'

For a moment Heaton looked obstinate, then he gave way and led Harry into the room at the back of the shop which was half parlour and half office. He pulled forward a seat for Harry, but sat himself on the edge of a table from which he could see through to the shop door.

'I first saw her at the Plough about three months ago. She was often hanging about there, trying to pick up some man who would buy her drinks or a meal. Then about a month ago she came in here to buy a cat and since then she's been in several times. She's actually a very good customer. Oddly enough she seems to have money to burn – at the moment, anyway.'

'Have you ever met a friend of hers called Judy Black?'

'No, never,' Heaton said hastily. 'But then I wouldn't. I don't know any of her friends. I've just told you. She's not really a friend . . .'

'But you had dinner with her last night,' Harry persisted mercilessly.

'Yes. We did last night but . . .' Heaton launched into a complicated series of excuses. Harry listened with patience and then interrupted quietly.

'Where does she live?'

Heaton stopped dead. 'Where – does she live?'

'Yes.'

'She has a flat in Defoe Mansions.'

'Where's that?'

'It's on the Carrington Road.'

'Have you been there?'

'No, never.' Heaton tried to meet Harry's steady stare but his eyelids flickered and he turned his face away. 'Well – once.'

'Only once, Mr. Heaton?'

'Well – er – twice, as a matter of fact.'

'What number Defoe Mansions?'

'Thirty-two, I think it is.'

If Heaton had confessed to the murder of Mrs. Rogers he could not have looked more guilty or ashamed of himself. He had picked up a dog biscuit which lay on the table and was crumbling it in his fingers.

'Thank you, Mr. Heaton,' Harry said. He pushed through the curtain and walked the length of the shop. When he opened the door a bell pinged in the little room where Sidney Heaton still stood, his eyes cast down to the ground.

Defoe Mansions was a humbler building than its high-sounding name suggested. Originally three nineteenth-century houses, the interior had been ruthlessly hacked about to provide a number of flats, which the sales brochure had described as 'ultra-modern' and 'luxury'. The entrance was in the central house and from the front hall a lift gave access to the upper floors.

Marty Smith emerged from the lift and paused in the hallway to light a small cigar. He was wearing a new check sports jacket and there was a self-satisfied expression on his pock-marked features. The tick which contorted the right side of his face when he was under stress was quiescent at the moment.

He flipped the match on to the polished lino floor and sauntered out into the sunlight of the morning. Across the street and a hundred yards up the road was a boozer which he often used. He reckoned he'd earned himself a pint.

He had crossed the street and was heading towards the Rose and Crown when his suspicious eyes spotted a car slowing down opposite Defoe Mansions. He moved into a shop doorway to watch. The green Austin 1100 found a parking space and as the driver turned to reverse into it, Marty recognised the face. An involuntary flicker jerked his right cheek.

He waited till Harry Dawson had entered the building, then crossed the road slowly at a point where he was not visible from the hallway. By the time he entered the hall the lift was on its way up. Marty watched the numbers on the indicator glow as the lift passed the second floor and stopped at the third. Just to make sure, he pressed the call button and the lift began to come down.

No doubt about it, Dawson had got out on the floor where Linda lived.

Three minutes later Marty was in the public telephone booth at the Rose and Crown. He dialled a number which he knew by heart. While it rang he twisted round to make sure that no one was near enough to hear what he said through the walls of the booth. The voice answered almost before he was ready for it.

'Tam? This is Marty . . . Listen, I'm outside Linda's place, I've just delivered the passport . . . No, no, she's okay. But listen to this! I've just seen Harry Dawson . . . No, two minutes ago . . . Yes, he's just gone into her apartment.'

Marty took out a grubby handkerchief to wipe his brow. Talking to Tam always made him nervous.

'Well, I hope she does play it cool . . . What? This is a hell of a line . . . Yes, you do that, you phone her, that's a very good idea. Okay, Tam.'

Relieved that he had shed the responsibility, Marty hung up the receiver. He was stroking the right side of his face as he came out of the booth.

Harry had needed to ring several times at the door of flat number 32 before he heard an impatient voice calling: 'All right, all right, I'm coming.' The door was opened by the woman he had seen twice before. She was wearing a fur coat and her handbag dangled from her forearm.

'For Gawd's sake . . .!' she began to remonstrate. She stopped dead when she saw who was standing there.

'Good morning, Miss Wade,' Harry said, putting on his most friendly smile. 'You remember me, perhaps? I'm Detective Inspector Dawson. We met in the Golden Plough last night. Could you spare me a few minutes?'

Behind her calculating eyes Linda Wade's mind was working fast. 'Well, it's a bit awkward at the moment. I was just going out. I've got an appointment at the hairdresser's at half-past eleven.'

Harry kept the smile going. 'It'll only take a few minutes.'

'Well—'

'You look to me more as if you'd just come *back* from the hairdresser's.'

Linda patted her suspiciously lustrous red hair. Even in these circumstances she could not help being flattered by the compliment.

'Nonsense! It's in a frightful mess.'

'May I come in?' Harry moved forward, following up his advantage. 'Just for a moment.'

'Yes, okay. But I warn you it will only have to be for a few moments.'

The flat was over-heated. Harry felt the warmth hit his face as soon as he entered the hall. The interior was a surprise, totally at variance with the external appearance of Defoe Mansions-. The immediate impression was that the owner had walked into one of those antique shops which specialise in gilt mirrors and highly ornamental *objets d'art* and just bought the lot.

'What a beautiful flat!' Harry said, as Linda closed the door behind him.

'Do you like it?'

'I do. I do indeed.' Harry was looking around him as he walked towards what was obviously the sitting-room. He was noting the position of doors, searching for any object which might have been carelessly left lying around.

The sitting-room had one of the large bay windows which had been a feature of the original house, and the ceiling was high. A pair of double doors, at the moment ajar, led through into the bedroom.

No money had been spared on this room. A purple carpet stretched from wall to wall. A wide divan jutted from one side of the room, adorned with a tiger-skin rug and a scatter of gaudy cushions. The arm-chairs were deep and welcoming, the desk secretaire had obviously cost a bomb and there were large mirrors on every wall. The dominant feature was a large, very modern cocktail cabinet.

Yet the whole effect was impersonal. There was nothing here to awaken guilty memories of home in the male visitor's mind. It was an ornate kind of reception room.

'I'm sorry I can't offer you a drink, there really isn't time,' Linda said. She had not invited him to sit down.

'Miss Wade, I'll tell you why I wanted to see you—'

'I think I know why, duckie,' Linda cut in. 'About Judy Black?'

'Yes.' Harry did not show his surprise at her coming to the point so quickly.

'I nearly phoned you last night, after I'd seen you in the Plough, and then I thought – you keep out of this, Linda. Don't get mixed up in anything. You've always been a good little girl – with reservations, of course – you keep it that way, sweetie.'

There was something rather engaging about her frank way of talking.

'But you do know Judy?'

'Yes, of course I know her. Don't know her very well but—' She paused, then looked him in the eye. 'She stayed the night with me, the night Newton died.'

'Where is she now?'

'I don't know, duckie. And that's the truth. Honestly, I don't know.'

There was a faint tang of cigarette smoke in the air and half a dozen cork-tipped cigarette ends had been crushed in the Venetian glass ash-tray; some of them had been only half smoked.

Harry took out his case and offered it to Linda.

'I don't smoke, thanks. But you go ahead.'

Harry lit up and then turned to her appealingly. 'Look. I'm going to be frank with you. I'm in a spot. I've got to find Judy and I've got to find her before—'

'Sweetie, I've just told you, I don't know where she is. I haven't a clue. I haven't seen her since she did a bunk that night.'

'Is that the truth?'

Linda drew her scarlet-tipped finger across a well-defined bosom. 'Cross my heart—'

Harry allowed his eyes to be drawn to the cleavage between her breasts. He smiled wryly in acceptance of her statement and gave her arm a squeeze.

'Okay . . . Okay, I believe you.'

Confident now that like all men he had become more interested in her physical attributes than anything else, Linda reacted to the squeeze with a little squirm of sensuous pleasure.

'In any case, you're barking up the wrong tree. She didn't kill Newton. He was her meal ticket, so why should she kill him?'

'They had a row that night.'

'So what?' Linda laughed. 'I'm always having rows but I haven't knocked anybody off. Not yet.'

'Did you know Newton?'

'Yes. I knew him.' Linda turned the corners of her mouth down. 'Didn't like him very much. Altogether too much of a smoothie for my liking. Always used to think he was a queer, as a matter of fact, but turned out he wasn't.'

'Well, I'm sorry you can't help me.' He nodded towards the bar. 'Sorry about the drink too. Some other time, perhaps?'

'Why not? We're always open!'

'Open to offers?' Harry suggested.

'I meant the bar.' Linda pretended to be mildly shocked, then put on the come-hither expression she had been wearing when she took Sidney Heaton out of the Golden Plough. 'But we're open to offers too, sweetie.'

Harry echoed her, laugh and bent to stub his cigarette out in the ash-tray. He moved out into the hallway.

'I'll drop in again, if I may. One evening, perhaps? *After* you've been to the hairdresser's.'

'You do that. But give me a ring first. And I'm sorry I could not be more helpful – about Judy, I mean. But you're wasting you time, duckie, you really are. She didn't kill Newton.'

Harry stopped and turned round. In the sitting-room the telephone had started to ring.

'Then who did?'

'I don't know, but it certainly wasn't Judy. Listen, I must answer that phone.'

'All right. I can let myself out.'

'See you.'

Linda started towards the living-room. Harry put his hand up to twist the knob of the Yale lock and as he did so he slipped up the button which would put it on the latch. Turning at the door of the living-room, Linda was able to see the door of the flat close on him.

Outside on the landing Harry stood for a moment, holding the door to by the handle of the knocker. He could faintly hear Linda's voice and knew that she was now at the telephone, but he could not hear what she said.

He pushed the front door open, re-entered the hall, quietly released the latch and closed the door. He could now quite clearly hear what she was saying.

'He's just left . . . Yes, I did . . . It would have looked a hell of a lot fishier if I hadn't asked him in . . . No, I played it cool . . . What? . . . Well, she's all right, but a bit nervous . . . Yes, I think it's very good, the photograph's excellent . . . No, he didn't. I'm picking the ticket up myself . . . Tam, listen . . .' Linda's voice became pleading. 'Do you always have to send Marty? Couldn't it be someone else, just for once? . . . Do I like him? He's a flaming monster!'

Harry sensed that the conversation was coming to an end. He cautiously opened one of the doors leading off the hall. It was a bathroom. He slipped inside and pushed the door till it touched the jamb but did not click shut.

Linda had finished her telephone call. He could hear her footsteps on the floor of the hall outside. She seemed to be fussed about something. Harry guessed that she was searching for her handbag or her purse. Once she came right up to the door of the bathroom and he could hear her muttering to herself.

Then she changed her mind and his heart-beats slowed down again. A few seconds later he heard the front door close.

He gave her half a minute, then pulled his door open and slipped out into the hallway. Beyond the door of the flat the lift doors clattered.

Although he was now the only person in the flat some instinct made him move cautiously and silently. He stood for a moment in the centre of the living-room letting his eyes roam methodically around. 'Give your eyes a chance,' was a well-known police adage.

The Venetian ash-tray was the first item to receive his closer scrutiny. He picked up one of the tipped cigarettes he had noticed. It was a Piccadilly, the brand which Judy Black had been smoking that night in St. James's Park.

Next he moved to the desk. He quickly opened and shut a number of drawers, rifling rapidly through their contents. In the fourth drawer he found what he was looking for, a British passport. He took it to the window.

The number was N 35645, which indicated that it had probably been issued about five years ago. The name in the panel at the top was Miss Stella Morgan. He turned to the third page where a photograph had been pasted into the square marked 'bearer'. The face was familiar, yet strange. The features were those of Judy Black, but the hair was dark and arranged in a completely different, rather severe style. She was wearing heavy horn-rimmed glasses.

'Judy.'

Staring at that face whose attractive innocence shone even through the harsh passport photograph, he realised that he had involuntarily spoken her name aloud.

He was examining the page headed 'Description/Signalement' when he thought he heard a faint noise from the adjoining bedroom. It had sounded like somebody stealthily opening a sash window.

He slipped the passport into his jacket pocket and moved swiftly to the bedroom door. It had been ajar while he was talking to Linda and he thought it had been opened slightly.

He thrust the double panels of the door away from him with such force that they swung back and hit the walls behind. In one quick sweeping glance he took in the features of Linda's bedchamber, or at least the chamber which she used when she was entertaining guests – the broad divan bed, the huge wardrobe with the swinging mirror door, the heavy shaded table lamps, the suggestive pictures on the walls.

But it was the window which riveted his attention. The bottom half had been pulled right up and a faint breeze was blowing the frilly curtains out into the room. He crossed to it quickly and leaned out.

The low sill gave on to an iron fire-escape erected at the back of Defoe Mansions. Three storeys below, in the back yard of the Mansions, two cars and a van were parked. There was no one on the fire-escape.

Craning his head to look upwards he saw that the stairway finished at roof level only one storey above him. He scrambled quickly over the sill and ran up the remaining two sections to the roof.

The roof of Defoe Mansions was flat, broken by chimney stacks and those humped-shaped columns which contain a door leading to the house below. They were probably no longer used but none the less they provided plenty of hiding places.

He walked slowly along the roof, taking care not to trip over pipes, odd bricks and patches of roofing felt. If he quartered the roof methodically he would force anyone hiding there to change position. And if he kept the top of the fire-escape under surveillance they could not escape. The roof of Defoe Mansions was high above the houses flanking it.

As he reached the end of the roof and turned to come back along the other side he heard a sound like someone tripping over a loose plank. He spun round and caught a flash of colour as a figure moved behind a chimney breast.

Harry moved fast now, like a hawk that has spotted the quarry. He came round the end of the chimney stack and pulled up short.

Judy was standing at the edge of the roof, a foot-high parapet separating her from the drop beyond. Her dark tinted hair hung down at the side of her pale face. Behind the plain glass lenses of her spectacles her eyes were wild. She was panting, either with fear or the exertion of her climb, and in her hand she clutched a small, snub-nosed automatic.

Harry stood very still, not so much for fear of the gun, though

99

she looked perfectly capable of using it, but for the fear that if he advanced she might step back and go over the edge.

'Hallo, Judy.' He spoke in a conversational tone, his arms hanging limply at his sides.

She did not answer. Beyond her the backcloth of roofs and chimney stacks was sharply outlined by the sunlight.

'You're getting careless, you know, leaving such obvious traces of yourself in Linda's flat. And this too—' He pulled the passport from his pocket. 'It's not a very good photograph, is it? Still, it's not a very good passport either, if it comes to that. Who gave you this useless piece of cardboard, Judy? Tam Owen, was it?'

'Give it to me,' Judy said tensely.

'Sure.'

Harry tossed the passport on to the ground between them. To pick it up she would have to move away from the edge of the roof. So long as she stood where she was he dared not try to rush her in case she involuntarily stepped backwards.

She came forward and stooped to pick up the passport, but the gun barrel never went off aim. In her highly emotional state of mind she was probably quite capable of pulling the trigger, so all he did was move slightly to her flank.

He said: 'Do you know what I'd do with that, if I were you? I'd burn it.'

'I'm not interested in what you would do with it.'

'Aren't you, Judy?' Harry took another step sideways. He nodded at the gun. 'Is that the gun you shot Peter Newton with?'

'I didn't shoot Peter.'

'Then why are you running away?'

'Don't you know why?'

'Yes. I know. You're running because someone has convinced you that we're going to charge you with the murder, whether you did it or not. It isn't true, Judy. I told you the other night, if you tell the truth you've nothing to worry about.'

The heavy glasses were a size too big for her. They kept slipping down the bridge of her nose and every now and again she had to put up a hand to push them back.

'I don't believe you. Even if you accepted my story, Nat Fletcher wouldn't.'

'Why shouldn't Nat believe you?' Harry was genuinely puzzled by her statement.

Judy ignored his question. 'I want you to go back down to the flat now.'

'Judy, listen to me! I took a risk the other night when I agreed to stop that taxi and—'

'You heard what I said.' Her voice had a hint of hysteria in it. She was gripping the gun so tightly that her knuckles were white. 'Go back!'

Harry let his shoulders slump in defeat. 'I hope you know what you're doing,' Judy. If you use that passport and *then* we pick you up—'

'Do as I tell you!' Judy almost shouted. 'Go back to the flat!'

Harry gave a hopeless shrug.

'All right, Judy,' he said submissively.

As he turned away he saw her free hand move to readjust her spectacles. He chose that instant to turn and launch himself at her, hoping to deflect the barrel of the gun downwards before she could press the trigger.

For a fraction of a second she hesitated, surprised by his sudden move or perhaps in her heart of hearts reluctant to carry out her threat. Then she closed her eyes and pulled the trigger.

The automatic leaped in her hand, surprising her by its re-coil. The report, so close to her ears, seemed deafening. She opened her eyes and saw Harry crashing to the ground at her feet. In horror she recoiled backwards. The low parapet was waiting to trip her by the legs. As she felt herself begin to lose balance she grabbed wildly at the air in front of her for support. For a split second she was outlined against the sky like a crazy-marionette jerked on the end of a string. Then she toppled backwards over the edge of the roof, and as she fell her scream of terror floated up from below.

Chapter 3

It was the sound of the sirens that made Marty Smith put down the remains of his pint and hurry out into Carrington Road. A couple of fire engines, a police car and an ambulance tore past in quick succession. Opposite Defoe Mansions a crowd had collected on the pavement and were staring upwards.

Marty followed their line of sight and a shiver of pleasurable excitement ran through him. High up on top of Defoe Mansions he could make out the shape of two people, a man and a woman. They were clinging, or rather the man was clinging to the ridge of a dormer window in the roof of the new section which had been added when Defoe Mansions was converted. With his free hand the man was holding the waist-belt of the woman. By the lifeless way her body was slumped she must be either unconscious or dead.

Marty could see what had happened. She must have fallen from the main roof and slithered down the roof of the extension. If the dormer window had not been on the line of her fall, she must have plunged to the pavement far below. There was only one way the man could have reached her. He must have slid down the roof after her.

The mere thought was enough to make Marty shiver. He moved closer.

The fire brigade wasted no time in running an extending ladder up to the dormer window. The helmeted fireman, assisted by the man on the roof, got the woman over his shoulder and began to descend. The man edged over until he could get a foot on the top rung and then descended after them. The police had to hold the crowd back as the inert body was placed on a stretcher and swiftly loaded into the ambulance. The white vehicle, its blue light flashing and siren sounding, dashed away up the street.

Pushing reporters, police and onlookers aside, the man who had been on the roof raced towards a green Austin 1100 parked by the kerb. He jumped inside and set off in pursuit of the ambulance, whilst the police patrolmen piled into their own car to follow.

A buzz of excited speculation rose from the astonished onlookers. Marty Smith ran for the Rose and Crown, feeling in his pocket to see if he had the coins he would need for the telephone.

'For heaven's sake, relax, Harry! They've already told you she's going to be all right.' Nat spun the upright chair round and sat down, straddling it with his legs and leaning his arms on the back frame. 'My God, if I were you I'd be out celebrating instead of worrying about a little tramp that tried to shoot the hell out of me.'

Harry said nothing. Nat glared at him accusingly and then pointed in the direction where they both knew the mortuary was.

'*You* could be out there, chum. Don't you realise that? If you hadn't reacted quickly enough to dive under the bullet you could be out there lying on a slab for all she cares.'

Harry was leaning with his back to the radiator. He was too restless to sit down and in any case the chairs in the hospital waiting-room were not very inviting. He had reached the hospital in time to see Judy being taken through the doors of the casualty department. The vague reassurances of the doctor on duty had not allayed his anxiety and he had decided to sit it out till she recovered consciousness. Within ten minutes Nat had joined him in the waiting-room.

'Yes, I know,' Harry said, his expression still obstinate. 'I know that's what it must look like, Nat. But I'm sorry. I don't share your opinion of this girl. I never have done.'

Nat's face registered his amazement. 'What *is* this, Harry? Are you falling for her?'

'Don't be a damn fool!'

'Well, are you?' Nat rose angrily from the chair. 'Let me tell you something about this outfit. Let me really put you in the picture. Ever since those photographs were found I've been checking up on Mister Peter Newton and Miss Judy Black.'

Nat came up close to Harry, almost as if he was putting the pressure on one of his own subjects.

'Sergeant Quilter and I must have talked to half the prostitutes in London, to say nothing of the ponces. We're up to our eyebrows in sex, Quilter and me. Right now, my idea of a swell night out would be a nice juicy apple and a couple of hours Bingo.'

'What did you find out about Judy?'

'Newton worked for a man called Tam Owen.' Nat turned and began to pace the room. 'Don't ask me who Tam is because I don't know. Ostensibly he works the usual call-girl racket but in fact there's more to it than that. A wealthy man comes to Town in search of fun and games. He calls a certain number and talks to a charming girl called Judy Black. She finds out who he is and passes him over to Peter Newton – or rather she did. Newton provides the glamour pants and within twenty-four hours the poor sucker finds himself buying a very nice set of highly revealing photographs from our Mr. Owen.'

'You're forgetting that it was Judy who first told us about Tam Owen. Why should she do that if she was part of the set up?'

'It's pretty obvious why. She thought she had the skids under her and she was frightened of you, Harry.'

'I don't agree. It's not me she's frightened of, Nat. It's you.'

'Me?' Nat halted in his pacing and stared at Harry in astonishment. 'But I've never met the girl.'

'Never?'

'No, never. What makes you think I have?'

'It's not important.' The window opposite Harry looked across to a corridor running parallel to the building they were in. He could see two male nurses pushing a mobile stretcher towards the operating theatre, but the person lying on it was below his line of sight. 'The thing is, where do we go from here?'

'How to get a lead on this bastard Owen, that's our problem. And don't think that Judy Black is going to talk, because she isn't. Owen has put the fear of the devil into her.'

'There's always Linda Wade,' Harry suggested quietly.

'You know what your friend Heaton said about Wade,' Nat pointed out. 'She's got money to burn. That money's coming from Tam Owen. She's not going to kill the golden goose, Harry.'

'I wonder.'

'Well, if you think you can make an impression on Miss Wade, go ahead. Talk to her. Anything's worth a try.'

Nat stopped as the door was opened. A doctor who seemed extraordinarily young to Harry's eyes came in. He was not the doctor whom Harry had seen earlier.

'Inspector Dawson?' He was looking enquiringly at the two men.

'I'm Dawson,' Harry said, stepping forward.

'My name is Friedman. I will be looking after Miss Black—'

'How is she, doctor?'

'She was very lucky, sir. I think she may have been knocked unconscious when she went over the parapet so that her body was limp when it struck the ridge of the dormer window which you described. That contributed to avoiding a severe fracture. In fact, her shoulder was dislocated but we have re-set it and there should be nothing to worry about there.'

'Can I see her?'

'Well—' The doctor pursed his lips and looked dubious. 'She started asking for you when she recovered consciousness. But she has had a very nasty shock and we've given her a sedative. It would be better if you could call me back later in the days and we'll see how she is. Could you make it fairly late, we'd like her to get as much sleep as possible?'

'You name the time, doctor.'

'Would eight o'clock be convenient?'

'Yes – that's fine.'

The doctor nodded and turned to the door. The attentive, concentrated manner of the two police officers seemed to have made him uneasy.

When he had gone Nat started buttoning his overcoat. 'I'll meet you here at five to eight, Harry.'

Harry nodded. His thoughts were elsewhere. 'All right, Nat.'

'I mean what I said about Linda Wade.' Nat spoke in a more friendly tone. 'Give it a try.'

The rush-hour had not started when Harry drove back in the direction of Defoe Mansions. This time he parked a couple of hundred yards up the street and proceeded the rest of the way on foot.

Opposite the Mansions he paused for a minute, looking up at the roof and re-living those moments when he had looked over the edge of the parapet, expecting to see Judy's body crushed on the pavement below. From down here the ridge of the dormer window hardly seemed sufficient to arrest a falling body. He had almost missed it himself when he had slithered down the roof to reach her.

A movement at the entrance to the flats drew his attention back to street level. A man had come out, almost at a run. He was wearing a corduroy Norfolk jacket and a silk neck-scarf. Harry recognised him at once as Sidney Heaton. Throwing glances up and down the pavement, he made for a Singer Gazelle parked on the Defoe Mansions side of the road. His hands were so unsteady that he had difficulty inserting the key in the lock and when he pressed the self-starter the car jumped forward because he had forgotten to take it out of gear.

When he did succeed in getting the engine going he swung out into the street without checking his mirror and accelerated hard past the Rose and Crown.

Harry watched the car till it disappeared, then walked swiftly across the street.

He was alone in the lift as it climbed to the third floor, and when he closed the doors the cage remained where it was. The door of Linda Wade's apartment, he saw at once, was slightly open.

He stood on the door-mat, trying to identify the sound which he could hear from inside. Then he slowly pushed the door open and went inside.

He realised at once that what he had heard was a woman

uncontrollably sobbing. The sound was coming from a room opposite the bathroom where he had hidden. He tip-toed to the threshold and found himself looking into a more intimate and personal bedroom than the one opening off the sitting-room.

Linda Wade was sitting at her dressing-table, facing her make-up mirror. She was mopping with a hand-towel at the tears which were streaming down her face. Her shoulders were bare except for the straps supporting her brassiere and her flesh was scored by angry weals, some of them so deep that they were oozing blood. Somebody must have beaten her up viciously with a riding crop or dog whip.

Used as he was to sights of violence, Harry could not help feeling sickened by what he saw. He walked tentatively towards her. She caught the movement in her mirror and slowly turned round.

'How the hell did you get in?'

'Oh my God!' Harry whispered. Linda's attacker, not con-tent with beating her about the shoulders, had slashed her across the face. The wound disfigured the whole left side of her face from temple to chin.

'Yes,' Linda said, still shaken by the sobbing which she was powerless to control. 'Pretty, isn't it?'

'You need a doctor!' Harry moved towards the telephone but she put out a hand to stop him.

'I don't want to see a doctor. I don't want to see anyone. I never want to show my face again.'

She buried her face in the towel.

'Who did this?' Harry asked in a dangerously quiet voice. 'Please leave me alone.'

'Linda, listen—'

'Didn't you hear what I said – leave me alone.'

Harry drew up a bedside stool and sat down beside her.

'I know who was responsible for this, you don't have to tell me. It was Tam Owen, wasn't it?'

Linda's sobbing checked momentarily. She looked up quickly at his reflection in the mirror, then switched to her own lacerated face.

'Oh, God ! Just look at me. Just look at my face. The swine!'

'Why did they do it? Because I found the passport? Because you slipped up over Judy?'

'Please leave me alone.'

At least the terrible sobbing had stopped. The anger which had replaced it was a good sign. He tried a different tack.

'Judy's in hospital. Did you know that?'

This time she swung right round, wincing at the pain in her shoulders.

'In hospital?'

'Yes. There was an accident.'

'I don't believe you.'

'It's true. She's in St. Matthew's.'

'Is she – badly hurt?'

'No. I don't think so. I'm seeing her tonight.' He pointed to her face. 'I know that looks pretty unsightly at the moment, but it's nowhere as bad as you think it is. You find yourself a good doctor and inside a couple of months there won't be a mark on you.'

'You're just saying that.'

Linda stared at her face in the mirror and gingerly put a finger up to touch the gash.

'No, I'm not, honestly. There's a plastic surgeon at St. Matthew's, he's supposed to be a wizard. I'll find out his name for you tonight.'

'Thanks.' Linda sniffed gratefully and then blew her nose on the towel.

Harry waited for a minute or so; then once again tried to persuade her to tell him who had given her this merciless beating up.

'Do you think I'm a fool?' she said, shaking her head. 'Can't you see what happened to me just because I made a mistake over Judy? I'm not telling you anything. In any case I don't know what you're talking about. I don't know anyone called Tam Owen. Oh, God! My face! I look awful.'

She had started to cry again.

'Sooner or later,' Harry said, 'you'll have to tell me about Owen, so you might just as well tell me now.'

'Please go away. Leave me alone. Please—'

It was obvious that she was still in too shocked a state to talk logically. Harry stood up.

'All right, Linda. We'll talk about this some other time. Is there anything you want? Anything I can do for you?'

'No, nothing. I'll have a couple of aspirins and go to bed for an hour.'

'Yes. That's a good idea.'

As he moved to the door Harry allowed his eyes to explore the small bedroom. He could see nothing that might have been left behind by a visitor.

'By the way, how long did Mr. Heaton stay with you?'

'Heaton?' Linda's surprise seemed perfectly genuine.

'Yes.'

'I haven't seen Heaton. He hasn't been here.'

'Hasn't he, Linda?'

She did not answer. She was dabbing at her face again. 'Don't you think you'd better lock the front door after me, just to be on the safe side?'

She gave a little nod and stood up to follow him into the hall. He saw that her feet were bare. She had beautifully manicured toe-nails, painted gold.

The animals in their small cages instinctively picked up the mood of the customer who entered the shop in a state of such controlled anger that the air around him seemed to crackle. They set up a loud squawking, barking or gibbering which all but drowned the tinkling of the bell operated by the opening door.

The din brought Heaton from his own den at the back of the shop. 'We're closed. Can't you read the notice on the door?'

His voice was more petulant than angry. He was peering against the light to make out who his visitor was. Then abruptly his manner changed.

'Oh! Hallo,' Mr. Dawson.'

'I want to talk to you, Heaton,' said Harry unceremoniously.

'Yes. Yes, of course.' Heaton began nervously to rub the back of one hand with the other. 'I – er, I'm afraid I didn't recognise you. Would you like to come into my little parlour?'

Harry ignored the invitation.

'What happened this afternoon?'

'This afternoon?'

'Yes. At Miss Wade's.'

'I'm so sorry.' Heaton nervously tucked the scarf at his neck further under his striped shirt. 'I'm afraid I don't understand.'

'Then I'll spell it out for you. I want you to tell me, quite simply, what happened this afternoon when you went to Linda's flat.'

'I think there's some mistake, Mr. Dawson.' Heaton was trying to meet Harry's accusing stare. 'I spent the entire afternoon here, working on my accounts.'

'No good, Heaton.' Harry shook his head. 'I saw you. You came out of the Mansions. You had trouble getting the key into the lock of the Gazelle's door and you tried to start up while she was in gear. Now, who did you see there and what happened?'

'I – I didn't see anyone. I – oh, dear, this is almost embarrassing.' Heaton's mouth trembled and for a moment Harry thought he was going to burst into tears. 'I don't know quite what to say. I assure you, Mr. Dawson, I am not in the habit of visiting—'

'Look, Heaton, let's get one thing straight. I'm not with the Vice Squad. I'm not interested in your sex life. I don't care two hoots in hell who you sleep with, but there's one thing I want to know and I want to know it now. *What happened this afternoon?*'

Heaton stared at Harry like a hypnotised rabbit, then he brushed past him and went to the shop door. He shot a bolt and came slowly back.

'May I – start at the beginning?'

'No, I don't want to hear the story of your life. I just want to know what happened this afternoon.'

'I – I went to Linda's. It was a quarter past five when I got there.' Heaton ran his tongue over his lips. 'I let myself into the flat. I didn't realise what the noise was at first and then – She was in the living-room, on the floor, weeping. My God, she looked awful! Her dress was torn, there was blood on her face and shoulders.'

He covered his face with his hands and for a moment was unable to continue.

'She looked dreadful, Mr. Dawson, really dreadful. I just didn't know what to do.'

'What did you do?'

'I behaved very badly I'm afraid. But do try and understand my position, Mr. Dawson. There I was in a strange flat, with a woman like that, who'd been—'

'You bolted.'

'Yes. Yes, I'm afraid so.'

Harry did not allow Heaton's abject expression to soften him. He knew from experience that these apparently mild and cowed men are the ones most capable of sudden acts of horrific violence. Yet he could not bring _himself to believe that the frightened person he had seen fleeing from Defoe Mansions could have attacked Linda so brutally.

'Did Linda see you?'

'I don't know. I honestly don't know whether she saw me or not.'

'You said you let yourself into the flat.'

'Yes. She gave me a key.'

'She gave you a key? When?'

'Last night when we had dinner together. It was a sort of – well, receipt, you might say.'

'You'd paid her some money?'

'Er – yes. In fact I did. She gave me the key and told me I could use-it to let myself into the flat when I went to see her.'

Heaton reached into his trouser pocket and brought out a single Yale-type key. 'Here's the key.'

'Is this the truth you've told me?'

'I swear it is. I wouldn't lie to you about a thing like this, honestly I wouldn't.' Once again Heaton had put on his straight, honest look. 'You know me, Mr. Dawson.'

'That's just where you're wrong. I don't know you at all, Mr. Heaton.'

Harry reached out and took the key from his hand. 'I think I'll take that key.'

When Harry reached the hospital at five to eight Nat was already waiting for him, seated in the least uncomfortable of the chairs with the ankle of one leg propped on the other knee. He was enjoying a slow cigarette.

'It's a blessed relief to have a few minutes to oneself with no telephones ringing. I had ten minutes to spare so I came on here. Did you follow up the Linda Wade lead?'

'Yes, I did,' Harry said grimly. He told Nat about his visit to Linda's flat and his questioning of Heaton.

'I've never met Heaton.' Nat rose to stub out his cigarette on the outside sill of the partially opened window. There was a No Smoking sign in the waiting-room and therefore no ashtrays. 'It was Yardley who questioned him. But I must say his story sounds quite extraordinary to me.'

'Yes, but don't forget that I did see him leave the flat. He was really frightened, almost in a panic.'

'Could he have been putting on an act?'

'Yes. I suppose so. But why should he?'

'He'd just beaten her up, he was about to leave and then he suddenly spots you. So he pretends he's a frightened little man who hates violence and wouldn't hurt a fly.'

'It's possible, I suppose.' Harry was certainly not going to defend Heaton's character. 'But what's the motive? He's still got to have a motive.'

'Not necessarily. Maybe he's badly kinked and just did it for kicks. Girls like Linda Wade are frequently beaten up. It's a risk they take. It's all part of the game.'

Nat spoke with the cynicism that five years experience with the Vice Squad had given him.

'Yes, but there is another angle. Heaton could be working for Owen.'

Nat acknowledged this with a nod.

'Or alternatively,' Harry went on, pursuing a line of thought that had already occurred to him, 'you are right and he is putting on an act – a very big one.'

'Meaning?'

'Maybe Heaton is the man we're looking for. Maybe he is Tam Owen.'

'Well,' Nat sounded doubtful, 'that's possible of course.'

Nat was slowing in his reactions, Harty thought. It was not surprising. He had been working on the case for five days now and in that time two further murders had been committed. In those circumstances, day and night, weekdays and weekends made no difference. Till the murderer was caught there could be no rest, no respite.

'Nat, I've been thinking about Judy Black. If she does talk, if she is prepared to help us, we've got to take care of her. We can't just let her fend for herself when she's discharged from hospital. Not in view of what happened to Linda Wade this afternoon.'

'What have you got in mind, Harry?'

'Some friends of mine have a hotel in the Cotswolds. It's quiet, hidden away. No one need ever know she's staying there.'

'Where is this place?' Nat's eyelids were heavy. He was not really interested in what Harry was saying now.

'I've told you. It's in the Cotswolds. A village called Steeple Aston.'

'Okay.' Nat smiled at Harry, blinking sleepiness away. 'If she talks you have my permission to take her down there, but if she doesn't talk—' His tone changed. 'If she refuses to help us, then so far as I'm concerned that little miss has got to face up to – Oh, good evening, doctor.'

Nat jumped to his feet, slightly embarrassed. Doctor Friedman had opened the door behind him very quietly.

'Good evening,' the doctor said rather formally.

'How's the patient this evening?'

Nat's tone was breezy. The doctor quite deliberately turned to Harry.

'She's quite a lot better. She can leave tomorrow morning if she wants to but of course she will have to be careful for a day or two. I told her you were here, Mr. Dawson, and she'd very much like to see you, but—' Friedman glanced briefly at Nat. 'She'd rather see you alone, if possible.'

'That's okay,' Nat said, returning to his chair quite cheerfully. 'I'll wait.'

Judy was in a private room by herself. To Harry's surprise she was out of bed and sitting by the window in an arm-chair. She was fully dressed and her left arm was in a sling. She was smoking one of her inevitable cigarettes and was looking fairly well, apart from her pallor. It was still strange to see her with dark hair, but the heavy spectacles were nowhere in sight.

'May I come in?' Harry said, hesitating at the door.

She gave a little nod. He closed the door and drew up an upright chair.

'How do you feel?'

'Not – not too bad.'

'Is the shoulder painful?'

'No. It's all right at the moment.'

There was a short silence. Both of them finding it hard to say the right thing. Then Judy turned her head and for the first time looked at him.

'I'm sorry about what happened. It was my fault. I behaved stupidly, I realise that now. And they tell- me you risked your own life to save me.'

'There wasn't any risk really. The last thing I wanted was for you to get hurt.'

'What's going to happen now? What are you going to do with me?'

Harry sat down in the chair so that he was at an angle. He could see her in profile but she was not forced to look at him. He decided that she was well enough to hear what he had to say.

'Judy, I've got something to tell you. Linda Wade's been hurt. She – well, she was beaten up by someone.'

'No. Oh, no! When did this happen!'

'This afternoon. Her face is badly marked, I'm afraid.' He leaned forward in the chair and spoke quietly but earnestly. 'Now listen, you've got to tell me the truth. I want to know the truth about Newton and Tam Owen.'

'But I told you the truth!' Judy stubbed her unfinished cigarette into the ash-tray beside her.

'You said Peter Newton was in the property business. He wasn't. He and Tam Owen were running a call-girl set-up.'

Judy stared out of the window for a moment before answering. Then she said, very quietly, 'Yes. I know. Linda told me. She told me the whole story. I didn't know a thing about it, not until she—'

Impatiently she stood up and walked round behind him, out of his field of view.

'Oh, what's the use? You won't believe me anyway.'

'Tell me the story, then I'll tell you whether I believe you or not.'

Harry sat facing the way he was. She might open up more easily if she didn't feel he was pressurising her.

'According to Linda,' she began, 'when Peter first met me he intended that I should work for him, that's why he brought me to London. Then, when I'd been here for a little while he fell for me and decided that—'

She broke off for a moment. He heard her moving restlessly about behind him.

'I knew nothing about this call-girl business at that time. Peter kept all that hidden from me. I knew absolutely nothing about it and that's the truth.'

'But you knew about Linda,' Harry pointed out gently. 'You must have known the sort of life she was leading, otherwise—'

'Yes. I knew about her. She was a good friend to me. But I swear to you I didn't know about Peter.'

'What happened the night I picked you up outside the restaurant in Soho – the Chez Maurice?'

Judy, realising perhaps that she was still a bit weak on her feet, came back to her chair and sank into it.

'Tam Owen knew the police were looking for me and got one of his girls to tip you off. Then, when Linda saw you outside the restaurant she guessed what Tam was up to. She decided she must help me. So she phoned Tam and told him Peter had given me a letter – a letter containing information about him.'

'About Tam Owen?'

'Yes.'

Was that true – about the letter?'

'No. But it did the trick. He already had Marty Smith trailing me. When we stopped in the Mall Marty rang to check with him. Tam was worried in case I handed the letter over to the police—'

'So he told Marty Smith to mug me and bring you back to him. Then he talked you into skipping the country.'

'Yes. Except that it was Linda who did the talking. I've never met Tam Owen.'

'Never?'

'No, never. Only Marty. He's a friend of Linda's, although friend is hardly the right word. I don't think he's a friend of any-one's. In fact, he's the number One heavy in the Tam Owen set-up.'

She reached towards the open packet of cigarettes on the table beside her. Harry drew out his lighter and snapped it into flame. She put her hand over his to bring it closer to her cigarette.

'Go on, Judy,' he said, when she had expelled the first deep lungful of smoke.

'Linda told me if I stayed in this country I hadn't a chance. She said I'd already behaved so suspiciously that the police were bound to pull me in sooner or later. She promised to get me a false passport.'

'From Tam Owen?'

'Well, from Marty Smith. But it was done through Tam Owen.'

Harry pondered for a moment. Judy's face had gone paler. It was evident that this interview was taking its toll of her. But he had to make ground while the going was good.

'Judy, I've asked you this question before, but I'm going to ask you again. Did you kill Peter Newton?'

She looked him right in the eye and somehow this was quite different from Heaton's false stare. He had time to notice that she had very long eye-lashes under the high, arching brows.

'No, I didn't,' she said steadily.

'You didn't find out what he was really up to?'

'What do you mean?'

'You didn't discover that he was running this dirty racket and decide to take the law into your own hands?'

'No. I didn't.' Judy denied the accusation without exaggerated protestation. 'It wasn't like that a bit. I wanted to help Peter. I knew he was in trouble and I was trying to persuade him to go to the police about it. That's why we had that row in the restaurant.'

'But I thought you told me the row was about a dog collar.'

'It was. It was about the collar and the note. The note you received the morning after he was murdered.'

Harry moved his chair a little farther round so that he could see her better.

'Tell me about it, Judy.'

It was eleven o'clock the next morning when Harry picked Judy up from the hospital. Having been admitted as a casualty she had no luggage. The clothes she had been wearing had been cleaned and pressed by a sympathetic nurse. A good night's sleep had done wonders for Judy and the colour had come back into her cheeks. Her left arm was supported by a brilliant white sling and her jacket had been draped loosely over that shoulder.

The journey to Defoe Mansions did not take more than ten minutes. Harry made no attempt at concealment this time and parked his 1100 outside the entrance. The empty suitcase which he took from the boot would be full of Judy's things when they came down.

Outside the flat on the third floor he put the big suitcase down and gave her a reassuring smile before ringing the bell.

'Now, leave this to me. I'll talk to Linda. You needn't say anything. Just collect your things.'

She nodded and nervously adjusted the sling. After a minute Harry pressed the bell again and this time kept his finger on the button for ten seconds. They could hear it ringing inside the flat.

'I don't think she's in,' Judy said, hoping for the excuse not to have to confront Linda.

'It doesn't sound like it.' Harry nodded at the letterbox. 'Try calling her name. She might open when she knows it's you.'

Judy stooped and pushed open the flap of the letterbox.

'Linda,' she called through the aperture. 'It's me, Judy.'

Still there was no response from inside the flat. After another minute Harry took Sidney Heaton's key from his pocket and pushed it into the lock.

'Where did you get that?'

He ignored the question and quietly opened the door. He picked up the suitcase and walked into the flat, signalling for her to follow. He kept close behind her, just to be on the safe side, as she went into the sitting-room, calling Linda's name.

'She's definitely not here. My things are in this room—'

'Wait!' Harry stopped her as she put her hand on the door of a room facing the one where he had found Linda. He went past her to check the bedroom. It had an empty and abandoned look.

'All right,' he said. 'Pack your things as quickly as you can. There's something about this I don't like.'

Judy went past him and slid back the door of a built-in cupboard. Harry put the suitcase down on the bed and opened it.

'That's funny,' Judy exclaimed.

'What is it?'

'My things are here but Linda's seem to have disappeared.'

'Does she keep her stuff in here? I thought she—'

'No, a lot of it's in the other room, but she used to keep her long dresses in here. Wait a minute.'

Before he could stop her she had gone out of the room. He would have followed her but at that moment the telephone on the bedside table began to ring.

He stood looking at it for a moment, wondering whether to answer it or not. Then he picked the receiver up and put it to his ear.

Immediately a voice, said crisply: '586 1729?'

Harry glanced down at the disc to verify the number. 'Yes.'

'I have a telegram for Linda Wade.'

'Thank you. I'll take it.'

'Message begins: "Will expect you ten o'clock tomorrow". It's signed: "Douglas".'

'Douglas, did you say?'

'Yes, that's right.'

'Where was the telegram sent from?'

'It was handed in at St. Albans at eleven forty-five.'

'Thank you.'

'Do you want written confirmation?'

'Yes, please.'

Harry was still standing thoughtfully in front of the telephone when Judy returned.

'Who was that?'

'It was a wrong number. Have you discovered anything?'

'Yes. Linda's gone. She's left the flat. Her wardrobe's completely empty.'

Harry nodded. 'All right, Judy. Let's get moving. We haven't a lot of time.'

Judy moved to the wardrobe and began to fold her clothes and lay them in the suitcase.

'How long will it take us to get to this place?'

'It's about two hours to Bicester. Steeple Aston's about ten miles from there.'

Harry was standing in the middle of the room, once again letting his eyes conduct a quick but systematic search which took note of every detail.

'Steeple Aston?'

'That's the village. The hotel is called The Priory.'

'That's an unusual name for a hotel,' Judy said, returning to the wardrobe for another armful of clothes.

'Yes, I know. It's more a guest-house than a hotel. But don't worry. You'll like it all right.'

'Yes, I'm sure I shall. I'll be glad to get away from London.'

She folded a cardigan and placed it in the suitcase. Then she straightened up and looked at him across the bed. Her eyes had softened.

'I'm terribly grateful, Harry, for what you're doing.'

'There's no need to be grateful,' he said, thinking how very attractive she looked when she relaxed the rather hard manner which she affected. just take care of yourself. And, above all, remember what I told you. Don't give your address to anyone, don't go out of the hotel and if you must use the phone, phone me.'

She smiled at his emphatic and sincere tone.

'I'll remember that.'

'The people who own the hotel are friends of mine. I've told them that you're recovering from a nasty car accident and that you've got to be absolutely—'

He stopped and they both looked towards the hall. Someone had rung the door-bell. Harry put his finger to his lips and motioned Judy to stay where she was. He went out into the hall, closing the bedroom door behind him, and stood listening.

Outside on the landing he heard the clattering sound of the lift doors closing and then the receding moan as it descended. Whoever the caller had been his business was evidently not very urgent.

Just to make sure, Harry went and opened the door. The landing he looked out on was empty, but on the door-mat lay a long white envelope.

He stooped to pick it up. Even before his fingers touched it he realised that he had made an unpardonable mistake. The corner of his eye caught the movement of a trousered leg close to the wall flanking the door. He tried to twist sideways to avoid the blow which he knew must come. But he was too late. He never felt the gun-butt hit his head, never saw the floor coming up to meet his forehead.

Marty Smith stepped over the unconscious body and went quickly into the flat his gun at the ready.

'Judy!'

He stood at the entrance to the living-room, looking suspiciously round, then went to the doors of the adjoining bedroom and pushed them open. He came back into the hall, still calling her name. He saw the closed bedroom door and wrenched it open.

She was standing just inside, her eyes wide.

'Marty!' She managed to summon up a smile. 'It's you.'

'Yeah. Why the hell didn't you answer when I called.'

'I wasn't sure it was you. Did you manage to fix that stupid copper?'

'Sure.'

He took her by the arm and led her into the hall. She checked as she saw Harry's body lying in the doorway.

'Smug bastard had it coming to him,' she said. There was no trace now of the soft look in her eyes.

'Come on, Judy,' Marty urged her, as he led the way out on to the landing.

She had to step over Harry's body to follow. His head had turned sideways as he fell so that he was facing towards the lift. His eyes were shut, or almost so. She knew that he was not dead, only unconscious, for one eyelid seemed to twitch.

Marty was jabbing impatiently at the call button of the lift, even though the illuminated numbers on the panel showed that it was mounting. He had his hand on the door to open it as the lock was released. He hustled Judy in, thrusting the gun into his shoulder holster.

Mr. Pye was one of the longest established tenants in the Mansions and had a flat on the ground floor. He knew from experience that there was only one way of getting the lift to stop at the first floor when the passengers already in it had pressed the Ground Floor button; that was to pull strongly at the door so that it would open as the lift passed the trip.

The manoeuvre took Marty completely by surprise. He glared as Mr. Pye stepped into the lift, smiling amicably. He pressed the button for the ground floor and they all stood close together as the lift again began to sink.

Suddenly Judy, with her uninjured arm, made a grab for the gun in its shoulder holster. She managed to draw it out before Marty smacked his hand down on her wrist.

'Help me!' she shouted to the astonished Mr. Pye.

He reacted with surprising rapidity, flinging himself on to Marty's arm to keep the gun pointing towards the floor. It exploded a couple of times during the struggle sending bullets ripping through the floor and filling the confined space with the smell of cordite. Then Marty kicked Mr. Pye in the stomach. He gasped, loosened his hold and rolled on the floor.

At that moment the lift jerked to a halt. Marty opened the door and viciously pushed Judy out. She stumbled over the step and went staggering across the hall till she fetched up against the far wall. As Marty made to go after her, Mr. Pye reached a hand out and neatly tripped him up.

Swearing, Marty picked himself up and turned to aim another kick at Mr. Pye. Then he went for Judy, who had slid to the floor, almost fainting from the pain in her shoulder. He stooped to drag her to her feet, exposing his back to the staircase which reached ground level just alongside the lift.

Harry, racing the lift to the ground floor, was taking the steps three at a time. His final leap carried him right on to Marty's back, bearing him to the ground. The gun escaped from his fingers and Judy kicked it away across the parquet.

With sinewy strength Marty managed to break away from Harry's grip and roll clear. He bounced on to his feet like one of those toys that you can't knock over and almost at the same instant a knife appeared in his hand.

Harry just had time to get to his knees as Marty came in, but he knew that this was a position of advantage. As Marty lunged with the knife he pivoted sideways, slamming his left hand on the man's wrist. Then he brought his right hand across to meet Marty's using the other man's strength to drive the thrust upwards.

Marty howled and twisted over backwards to avoid his arm being broken. As he tried to rise a solid left from Harry's fist knocked him out cold.

Harry turned quickly to Judy, who was clutching her injured shoulder as she sat slumped against the wall. Her face was twisted with pain.

'Judy, are you all right?'

She managed to summon a brave smile.

'Keep on like this and they really will have to keep me in hospital.'

'You and me both,' Harry agreed, rubbing the new lump which he now had on the other side of his head.

Behind him Mr. Pye prudently collected Marty's gun from the floor and applied the safety catch.

Harry was taking things easy this morning. After all he was supposed to be on leave and he wanted to make the most of the days that remained. There was a lot to be done straightening out his father's affairs and there was always the shop to be looked after. Douglas Croft was competent enough, but he was reluctant to make decisions on his own. Now that he had presented them with Marty Smith, Harry felt that Yardley and Nat could get on with the job of smoking out Tam Owen. The suspicion which seemed to have been hanging over him at one time had been cleared up, though he was still not sure whether Yardley had been genuinely suspicious or not. If the Chief. Superintendent had seen that TV programme on his father, he might well have decided to put 'the tough little glamour boy of Scotland Yard' in his place.

Though he might not have admitted it to himself, however, the- principal reason for his feeling comparatively relaxed was the knowledge that Judy was safely hidden away where no one could find her.

He had telephoned her that morning, even before shaving and dressing. She had sounded happy and well. Even the rough and tumble with Marty Smith had not made her arm any worse. He repeated his warning about not leaving the hotel, not making any phone calls except to him.

He was just going into the bathroom to shave when the front door-bell rang. He hesitated, then decided he'd better answer it. It might be Nat with the latest developments. Maybe they had located Linda. It was even possible that Marty had been persuaded to break his obstinate silence.

The early morning caller was Hubert Rogers and to judge by his fresh, spruced up appearance he was on his way to the office. The tie was dead central in the V of the stiff white collar, the bowler on a safety level keel, the black shoes brightly polished. The rolled umbrella and brief-case were simply the finishing touches.

Harry could not quite conceal his surprise.

'Good morning, Mr. Dawson. Could you spare me a few moments?'

'Yes, of course, come along in.'

'I say,' Hubert was eyeing the silk dressing-gown and striped pyjamas with concern. 'I hope I haven't got you out of bed.'

'No. I've been up for some time,' Harry told him cheerfully as they moved into the sitting-room. 'I just haven't got round to getting dressed yet. I'm officially on leave, you know. Can I offer you anything?'

'No, thank you.' With typical predictability, Hubert laid his hat and umbrella down in exactly the same place as on his first visit. 'Dawson, I've been going through my aunt's things, dealing with her affairs and so on. Yesterday I had to make a decision about the dog.'

'Zero.'

'In the end I decided to take it down to a friend of mine who lives in the country.'

'Where was the dog? At the hotel?'

'Yes. Curiously enough they make provision for pets, that's probably why my aunt preferred the hotel in the first place.' Harry had noticed already that when Hubert spoke of his aunt it was with a certain condescension. Doubtless it rankled with him that he had a relation who stooped so low as to enter domestic service. 'Incidentally, you know it was all nonsense about her working there. She was actually staying as a guest.'

'Yes, I know.' Harry had no intention of inviting Hubert to sit down. 'But what was it you wanted to tell me?'

'Well, when I picked up Zero the first thing I noticed was his collar.' Hubert was opening the catches of his brief-case. 'It was obviously brand new and in view of the fuss my aunt made about the original one which your father gave her, I thought I'd take a jolly good look at this one.'

He took from the brief-case a brand new dog collar and handed it to Harry.

'Is there anything unusual about it?'

'Yes.' Hubert stood and waited for him to examine the collar.

It was made of a double thickness of soft leather. On the inside was a small zip fastener which ran nearly the full length of the half-inch wide strip.

'Was there anything in this pocket?' Harry said, slowly pulling the zip back to reveal the concealed pocket.

'Yes, there was.' Hubert was making the most of the situation. There was a faint air of triumph about him as he felt in his waist-coat pocket. 'Something belonging to you, Dawson.'

Harry took the slip of paper which Hubert produced and un-folded it. 'What is this?'

'It appears to be a receipt – for a pearl necklace.'

Harry unfolded the square of flimsy paper and smoothed it out on the table.

Minerva Jewels Ltd.
Burlington Street, Ref : A4961
London, W.1.

Dawson. Triple row graduated pearls. Restrung.

Harry looked up at his visitor. 'This isn't mine. But I can un-derstand how you thought it was.'

'But it's made out to you! It's got your name on it.'

'No. It's made out to my father. But I know all about it, Rogers. Thank you for bringing it to me.'

'You know all about it?' Hubert was crestfallen that his sur-prise had fallen so flat.

'Yes.'

'Do you mean, you knew my aunt had it? You knew it was in the collar?'

'No. But I knew the receipt existed. As a matter of fact, we've been looking for it.'

Harry's matter-of-fact tone was irksome for the other man.

'I see,' he said stiffly. Then suddenly his face reddened. 'No. I'm damned if I see!'

To disperse his burst of temper he walked to the window with quick little paces, then turned to face Harry. 'If the receipt belonged to your father, what was my aunt doing with it? And why hide it in the collar, for Pete's sake? And there's another thing. This collar's been specially made. You can't just walk into a shop and buy a collar like this, I'm jolly sure of that.'

'No, that's right. You can't.' Harry nodded his agreement but he was not really concentrating on what Hubert said. 'I'd like to keep this receipt and the collar, if I may.'

'Yes, of course, by all means.'

The little flare-up of temper had died quickly. Hubert coughed diffidently before he spoke again.

'Dawson, I spoke to Superintendent Yardley yesterday. He told me that there was nothing new on my aunt's murder and that there was no chance of an immediate arrest. But I had the feeling that he was, well – concealing something.'

'If he is, he's concealing it from me too.' Harry moved towards the door. 'Rogers, you'll have to excuse me. I have an appointment at half-past nine and as you see I'm not even dressed yet.'

When Harry came back into the living-room after showing Hubert out, he found Douglas Croft standing at the table, examining the dog collar. He had a folder under his arm and had come up from the office via the spiral staircase.

'Harry, what on earth is this? Where did this come from?'

'I'll tell you about that in a moment, Douglas,' Harry said briskly as he crossed the room to the telephone. 'I want to use the phone.'

'Is it private? Because if it is—'

'No, no.' There was a suggestion of a smile on his face as he began to dial the number. 'It certainly isn't private as far as you're concerned.'

Harry completed the dialling and resigned himself to waiting patiently for a reply. He glanced at Douglas and spoke casually.

'Douglas, do you know a girl called Linda Wade?'

'Linda – ?' Douglas was running the fastener of the zip on the collar back and forth.

'Wade,' Harry repeated.

'No. I don't think—'

'Have you heard of her?'

'Linda Wade. No, I haven't.' Douglas's face looked completely blank. 'Should I have done?'

Harry turned his back as a voice crackled in the receiver. 'Hallo, Telegrams? This is 586 2679. I want to send a message to Mrs. Sybil Conway, Stillwater, Broadway Avenue, Hampstead, London, N.W.3.'

He dictated the address slowly and clearly, listening to the tapping of the operator's typewriter at the other end. He could feel Douglas's eyes on the back of his head.

'Got that? The message is: "Have found receipt. Stop. Suggest we meet Serpentine Restaurant, Hyde Park, four o'clock this afternoon." '

He listened while the operator repeated the message, spelling the proper names. 'That is correct. The name of the sender is Croft. Douglas Croft.'

As the hands of his watch moved towards a quarter past four, Harry began to wonder whether the salmon was going to rise to the fly he had cast. Not that it was unpleasant sitting at his table on the terrace outside the Serpentine Restaurant. He could see couples in rowing-boats manoeuvring clumsily on the sparkling water of the lake, flocks of ducks and other water-birds crowding round a white-haired lady who had brought a bag of bread-crumbs down to throw to them. One of those lonely, isolated people who derive more pleasure from contact with creatures who cannot speak than with human beings. He could hear the subdued sound of cars on the road behind him. The park restrictions meant that those juggernauts with roaring and belching exhausts could not come within half a mile of where he sat. Beyond the trees across the Serpentine was the Hyde Park police station, its presence unsuspected by most users of the green space.

He spotted the Bentley as it swung round from the Ring Road. There were two persons sitting in the front seat. But Arnold Conway was alone as he came out on to the terrace. He looked very much the successful City man who has made his pile and retired at an early age. The check suit was well tailored, the wavy hair, greying only at the temples, had been cut by one of the best hairdressers.

He looked around for a few moments, noting that Harry Dawson was sitting there but that there was no sign of Douglas Croft. Then, without hesitation, he made for Harry's table.

'It was you who sent the telegram.' It was a statement rather than a question. Conway had sized up the situation and accepted it. 'You must excuse my wife. She wanted to get some shopping done, so I said I'd deputise for her.'

'It was you I was expecting, Mr. Conway.' Harry was vainly trying to catch the attention of a waitress before she disappeared inside the building. 'But you're a bit late. Did you have trouble parking your wheelchair?'

Conway's answer was an enigmatic smile and a question of his own.

'This telegram, Mr. Dawson. Was it fact or fiction?'

'I'm not sure I understand you. I have the receipt for the necklace, if that's what you mean.'

'That is what I mean. May I see it?'

Harry took the receipt from his pocket and held it up so that Conway could read it. The older man made no attempt to reach across and take it.

'Thank you,' he said. He took an oval-shaped cigarette from his case and lit it. The aroma of Turkish tobacco floated across the table. 'When did you first hear about this receipt?'

'Your wife got in touch with a friend of mine.'

'Douglas Croft.' Conway nodded. 'He used to work for your father.'

'That's right. Mrs. Conway telephoned Douglas. She said she thought my father had put the receipt away somewhere and—'

'She asked Croft to try and find it.'

'Yes.'

'And he found it?'

'No. Someone else-did.'

'I see.' Conway felt in his waistcoat pocket for a cigarette holder. 'But I still don't get the point of the telegram. Couldn't you have posted the receipt to my wife?'

'Yes. But in that case I would have been spared the pleasure of your company, Mr. Conway. And that wasn't what I had in mind.'

'What had you in mind? What is it you want?'

Conway had a way of dropping his eyelids when he looked directly at anyone. Harry leaned his elbows on the table, facing him.

'I want to know how my father got involved in this affair. I want to know why your wife started having an affair with him. I want to know why Tam Owen murdered him.'

Harry had spoken in a low voice and for a moment it seemed that Conway had not heard him. His expression did not change and his eyes did not flicker.

'Your father was a fool,' he said, equally quietly. 'And an unlucky one at that. My advice to you, young man, is don't get mixed up in this business.'

'Suppose I don't feel like taking your advice.' Harry made an effort to keep his voice down. He could feel the anger mounting in him.

'I can't imagine you'd be that stupid. You saw what happened to Linda Wade.'

'I don't scare that easily. I've seen people beaten up before, and I've had a few knocks myself.'

'I'm sure you have.' Conway blandly knocked the curving ash off his cigarette. 'But ifs not you I'm thinking of.'

'Who are you thinking of?' Harry asked. 'Judy Black?'

Conway showed his teeth in a suggestive smile. 'I'm sure you wouldn't like anything unfortunate to happen to Miss Black.'

'You're dead right. And nothing is going to happen to her!'

'You sound very confident. Is it because you don't think we could find her?' The smile had widened. Conway was genuinely enjoying himself. 'Would you like me to tell you where Miss Black is at this precise moment?

'Yes, I would. Go ahead.'

Conway took time to draw on his cigarette before playing

129

his trump card. 'She's at a hotel called The Priory. It's at Steeple Aston, a small village about ten miles from Bicester.'

The effect was not quite as Conway hoped. Harry's face broke into a wide grin. He leaned forward and patted the slightly padded shoulder.

'You wouldn't like to bet on that, Mr. Conway!'

The woman by the Serpentine had used up all her crumbs and lumps of bread. She addressed a few words of reproof to the ducks and drakes who had set up a loud chorus of protest at the signs of her departure, then turned her back on them.

For the first time since he had sat down Conway seemed less than totally sure of himself.

'What do you mean, I wouldn't like to bet on it?'

'Yesterday afternoon,' Harry explained briskly, 'I picked up Judy and took her to Linda Wade's to collect her things. While we were there Marty Smith showed up. I don't have to tell you what happened to Mr. Smith.'

'Go on.'

'After we'd dealt with Smith I went back and searched the flat. I found mikes and the tape-recorder. I knew it had recorded my conversation with Judy about the hotel at Steeple Aston, so I left the installation just as it was. I'm afraid it provided you with what our American friends call "a bum steer".'

'It didn't provide me with anything,' Conway said angrily, turning away so that he did not have to endure Harry's amused smile. 'I told Tam Owen a long time ago he'd be making a big mistake if he under-rated you—'

He broke off as a low, confidential, rather breathy female voice suddenly came through on the loudspeaker system. 'Will Mr. Cyril Conway please come to the reception counter to take an urgent telephone call. Mr. Cyril Conway, please.'

The system went dead the moment the announcement was concluded.

'It's for me,' Conway said in surprise. 'Where do I go?'

Harry pointed to a glass door at the end of the terrace.

'It's through there. There's a call box just inside.'

While he waited Harry amused himself watching a young man who had evidently never been in a boat before trying to emulate the winner of the Diamond Sculls. Conway was back within a few moments. He was like a cat on hot bricks, and his eyes were sending sharp, raking glances in all directions including the road running past the cafe.

'That was my wife,' he said, sitting down with assumed non-chalance. 'She wanted to know how long I was likely to be.'

'What did you say? Ten years?'

Conway tried in vain to show that he thought this an excellent joke.

'She said she'd come by in a few minutes.'

'Maybe she'd like to join us?'

'Frankly, old chap, I think she'd rather not—'

'The morning my father was murdered,' Harry interrupted very deliberately. 'It was Sybil he was expecting to meet at the club, wasn't it? She was the decoy. The refined, elegant, Sybil who he thought was in love with him.'

Conway did not have to reply. He cocked his head as he heard the familiar crackle which preceded an announcement on the public address system. The same breathy voice made its standard request.

'Will Mr. Harry Dawson please come to the reception counter to take a telephone call. Mr. Harry Dawson, please.'

'Your turn, old man.' Conway fitted a fresh cigarette into his holder as Harry stood up, hesitating as to whether he would answer the summons or not. Conway looked up and smiled. 'Don't worry, Inspector. I won't run away.'

Harry hurried along the terrace to the glass door he had indicated to Conway. Douglas Croft was the only person who knew he was here. Unless Mrs. Conway—

The girl at the reception desk looked up enquiringly as he approached the counter.

'Mr. Dawson? You can take the call in the kiosk over there.'

Before he went into the kiosk he glanced out through the door.

Conway was still there, sitting perfectly relaxed in his own private cloud of aromatic smoke.

He pulled the door shut behind him and lifted the receiver. All he could hear was the dialling tone. He tried speaking.

'Hallo. Dawson here. Hallo . . . Hallo.'

After half a minute he gave it up, opened the door, crossed to the reception counter and caught the attention of the girl who had spoken to him.

'There doesn't seem to be anyone on that line,' he said. 'Are you sure—'

A scream from out on the terrace interrupted him. It was followed by other screams and the sound of breaking glass as tables were knocked over.

Harry reached the door to the terrace in a couple of strides and wrenched it open. The tables round Conway were empty. The people had recoiled in the first instinctive moment of panic. Conway himself was not moving. He had slumped forward, his brow resting on the surface of the table.

Harry raced along the terrace. A quiet, professional-looking man, perhaps a doctor, had hurried up from the opposite direction. The two men reached the table at the same moment.

'What happened?' Harry asked.

'There was a shot,' the other said tersely. 'It came from somewhere up there.'

He gestured towards a clump of bushes near the road. Harry took Conway's hair and lifted the brow clear of the table. A pool of blood was forming from the bullet hole above his right eye.

He gently lowered the head then moved quickly off the terrace on to the grass where he could get a sight of the road behind the clump of bushes.

A grey Jaguar had pulled away from the kerb and was accelerating with smoking tyres. Defying the park speed restrictions, it disappeared in the direction of the Albert Memorial. There had been no possibility of reading its registration number.

Harry retraced his steps to the table where the dead man still sat. As he reached the terrace a woman in a fur coat came rushing out, her eyes wild and terrified. He moved quickly to intercept Sybil Conway before she could see what the bullet had done to her husband.

Harry stood on the pavement in Parliament Square watching the hands of Big Ben move up to and past eight o'clock. The evening rush-hour had ended and though the traffic swirling round the Square was heavy it consisted largely of private cars, taxis and privately hired buses bringing parties into London for an evening on the Town.

It had been difficult to fit a meeting into Chief Superintendent Yardley's very tight schedule. In the end Yardley had suggested this solution. He had to go up to Camden Town on another case he was investigating. If Harry joined him in the CID car they could talk during the journey.

It was seven minutes past eight when the inconspicuous blue Ford drew in to the kerb in front of him. Harry's heart sank. Yardley had released the police driver and was at the wheel himself. He was known as a terrifying driver.

The Superintendent leaned over to unlock the door on the passenger's side. He made no excuse for being seven minutes late as Harry settled in his seat and adjusted the seat belt.

'It's good of you to spare me some of your time, sir, especially at such short notice. I appreciate it.'

Harry's head jerked back as the clutch went in.

'Why did you want to see me?'

'I wanted to talk with you, but I thought if I came to the office there was a chance—' He broke off as the car made the sharp turn into Whitehall. 'I've found out the truth, sir, about my father.'

Yardley's grunt was encouraging enough for Harry to go on.

'This afternoon, after Arnold Conway was killed, I took his wife back to the house. She was in a terrible state. I let her talk. It would have been impossible to stop her anyway, even if I'd wanted to. She told me about my father and Mrs. Rogers. She explained why . . .'

'Dawson,' Yardley broke in. 'I'd like to hear what Mrs.

Conway told you, but don't you think you'd better start at the beginning?'

'Yes. I'm sorry.' Harry accepted the mild rebuke with a nod. 'Apparently before Mrs. Rogers worked for my father she had a variety of jobs and rather a chequered career, I'm afraid. One day she discovered that a man she used to work for – by the name of Tam Owen – was running a string of call-girls. She collected evidence of his activities – photographs, lists of contacts, a photostat of an incriminating letter he'd written. Then she started blackmailing him. At some point she must have realised the risk she was running, that Tam Owen was capable of killing her, so she told him that if anything happened to her my father, the famous Tom Dawson, would take over. In short, she inferred that she and my father were working together.'

'Which wasn't true.'

Yardley's method of negotiating the jumble of vehicles coming round Trafalgar Square was to steer a straight course for Cockspurs, keep his foot down and pretend there were no other cars on the road. The method worked, although several drivers angrily sounded their horns.

'No, of course it wasn't,' Harry resumed when the crisis was over. 'And even Tam Owen had his doubts about it. He told Sybil Conway to get friendly with my father and report back to him. Sybil reported that, in her opinion, Mrs. Rogers had lied. She also reported the fact that Mrs. Rogers was absolutely crazy about her poodle, Zero.'

'So they kidnapped the dog and offered to return it in exchange for the letter and photostat?'

The heater in the car had now started to function full blast. Yardley loved the fug and kept his window tight shut. Harry surreptitiously wound the window on his own side down a few inches.

'Right. Peter Newton – on behalf of Tam Owen, of course – telephoned Mrs. Rogers and they arranged to meet. That's when Mrs. Rogers made a note of the number of his car on one of the office folders which was lying on my father's desk. She met Peter.

They drove to his flat and he showed her the dog collar to prove that they really had got the poodle. But Mrs Rogers would not play because, unknown to Newton, it was the wrong collar. I'll be able to explain why when I've got some information out of Judy. The important thing is that Mrs. Rogers assumed that they were only trying to bluff her. So Tam Owen decided that he'd do something which would scare the living daylights out of her.'

'Like killing your father.'

The lights had gone red at the top of Lower Regent Street. Yardley braked to a stop, but kept the car in gear, riding the clutch with his hefty left foot. For a few seconds they sat and watched the almost hypnotic display of coloured lighting around Piccadilly Circus.

'Yes.' Harry continued his story in a quieter voice. 'Sybil Conway arranged to meet my father at the club for a golf lesson. Apparently she rang him to say she was delayed. She said she would meet him out on the course by the sixth green. Instead he was met by Owen and Marty Smith. Marty knocked him out and then Owen took a heavy stone from the brook and—'

Yardley glanced round with an expression of compassion on his face which Harry had not seen before. The lights changed and a taxi behind hooted impatiently.

'And Newton?' Yardley prompted, as he turned into Upper Regent Street.

'Newton was already on the course, all prepared to dash _ to the club-house with hit prepared story about his hooked drive hitting my father.'

'Well,' Yardley observed drily, 'people have gone to more extreme lengths than that to get away with murder. It all sounds most improbable but I must confess it ties in with what Judy Black told you. But I don't see why Newton sent you that note.'

'Newton didn't send it.'

'Then who did?'

'Judy did. You see, she'd guessed roughly what was going on. She felt confident that the best thing for Peter was for him to see me and make a clean breast of things. But she knew he never would unless someone or something forced him into it. Then she hit on the idea of sending me the dog collar and the note. That night she told Peter what she'd done and gave him the receipt for the registered letter. She told him that the very next day he'd be interrogated by the police and, if he had any guts, he'd tell them the whole story. Unfortunately they had a row. Peter went back to his flat and rang up Tam Owen. I don't have to tell you how Mr. Owen solved that problem.'

'No. You don't. My God, this bit of London gets more like the maze at Hampton Court every day!'

For the next few moments Yardley's whole attention was taken up with following the signs which led traffic round Oxford Circus and on to Portland Place.

'Isn't this going out of your way?' Harry asked him.

'I'll drop you at Regent's Park. It's a direct line from there

to St. John's Wood. You do want to go home, don't you?'
'Yes, thanks. That'll be fine.'

'Did she explain the business of the wheelchair and the cheque made out to Basil Higgs?'

'Well, the Conways were a very peculiar couple. They came into Tam Owen's racket mainly for kicks. Conway was the kind of man who bolsters up his own ego by watching other people making fools of themselves. He got a lot of amusement out of persuading a police officer to write a cheque in favour of one of the accounts they used to pay their blackmailing proceeds into.'

'And the wheelchair?'

'Did I tell you that Sybil Conway's excuse for stringing my father along without marrying him was this story about an invalid husband? Well, when I went to fetch Zero they had to play that out, didn't they? When I look back on it they must have been splitting their sides laughing. But it did have the effect of making you doubt my story, didn't it, sir?'

Yardley grunted and made no comment on that statement. The underground sign indicating the Regent's Park station had come into view before he spoke.

'You said you were going to explain something about the dog collar.'

'Yes. The collar was really symbolic of the suspicion and distrust of these people. Mrs. Rogers was the sort of person who's always on the lookout for material she could use to put pressure on people. She pinched the receipt my father had and hid it in Zero's collar.'

'But the dog didn't have a collar when you collected it from the Conways.'

'I know. All I can suggest at the moment is that he can't have been wearing it when he was stolen. Or somebody must have switched the collars.'

'And I suppose these pearls were valuable enough for Mrs Conway to want to get them back?'

'They were worth a bomb. That was what the thief who broke into Stillwater was really after. So she hit on the brilliant idea of trying to recover the value from the insurance company.'

'That's all very interesting, Dawson. But you haven't given me the answer to the most important question of all.'

'What's that, sir?'

Yardley pulled in to the kerb and sat frowning out through his windscreen.

'Who *is* Tam Owen?'

The police driver who brought Judy to Harry Dawson's flat next morning had been warned that if anything happened to her while she was in his care his career in the Metropolitan Police would come to an abrupt end. So he made her wait while he locked his car conscientiously and then stayed close to her as she crossed the pavement and climbed the stairs that led to the private entrance.

She pressed the bell and turned to him with a smile. 'I'll be all right now. Really I will.'

P.C. 387 was a cheerful-looking young man in his middle twenties. He gave her the benefit of his wide smile as he shook his head.

'My orders were to deliver you to Mr. Dawson personally, miss.'

His heart skipped a beat when he saw the smile which irradiated her face. But it was not for him. The door had opened and Harry Dawson was standing there. This time he was not in his pyjamas and dressing-gown. He was wearing a check sports jacket and a pair of tan slacks.

'Hallo, Judy. Come along in!'

'Good morning, sir,' P.C. 387 said, drawing attention to the fact that he still existed.

' Reluctantly Harry broke off the look which was passing between him and Judy.

'Good morning, Fuller. You can leave her in my care. And thank you very much.'

'It's been a pleasure.' Fuller grinned and turned to Judy. 'Any time, miss. Just ask the Inspector to give us a buzz. We can be very useful in the rush-hour.'

He smiled at Harry and departed down the stairs.

'What a smashin' bit of crumpet,' he was thinking. 'A beaut of a chassis and the nicest pair of legs in London. These CID boys certainly have it good.'

Harry was showing Judy into his sitting-room. It was a brilliant morning and the sun was pouring in through the windows. Judy had managed to wash the dark dye out of her hair and it glowed in the light. She had shed her sling and peemed to have no pain in the injured shoulder. He thought she looked simply great.

'Have you had breakfast?'

'Yes. I'd just finished when your driver arrived.'

Were you surprised when I phoned you?'

'Well, yes, I was.'

Harry led her to the part of the living-room where the easy-chairs were arranged. He had taken good care to clear his breakfast things out of sight.

'Sit down, Judy. Can I get you a cup of coffee?'

'No, thank you. Not just now.'

Judy sat down on the settee and tucked her legs up under her with cat-like litheness. Harry sat-himself at the other end.

'Judy, I had a long talk with Superintendent Yardley this morning. We want you to help us.'

'I'll do anything I can. I've already told you that.'

'Yes, I know, but – I want you to realise what you're doing, what you're letting yourself in for.'

Judy was pulling the cellophane wrapping off a new pack of Piccadilly filter-tips.

'What is it you want me to do?'

'First of all, we want you to talk to Linda Wade.'

'But I don't know where to find Linda. I haven't seen her since—'

'We've located Linda. Our indefatigable Sergeant Quilter ran her to earth in St. Albans.'

'St. Albans? What's she doing there?'

'She's in a private nursing home in Maylee Park where they specialise in plastic surgery. It's run by a very bright young surgeon called Douglas. Walter Douglas.'

Judy's brow wrinkled. 'Douglas? Where have I heard that name before?'

'The manager of my father's office is called Douglas. Douglas Croft. Quite a coincidence. Linda's due to have a grafting operation on her face tomorrow. Apparently, he takes a piece from one part of your anatomy and uses it to repair the damaged bit.'

Judy smiled. 'I can guess where they think Linda can spare it but I'll bet she's not going to like having a scar there either.'

'We'd like you to see her before she has the operation,' Harry said. She noticed that he had remained serious in spite of her little joke.

'All right, but if I know Linda, she'll be too frightened to talk. She won't say anything new. It's too late.'

'I realise that.'

'Then why do you want me to see her? What's the point?'

Harry waited while she pulled the little ribbon that brought the first cigarette out of the pack, put it in her mouth and lit up.

'We only want her to pass on a message. It's *you* we want to do the talking, not Linda Wade.'

'I'm damned if I understand you, Judy! I don't know what you're getting at!'

'I'm not "getting at" anything, Linda. I'm simply asking you to deliver a message for me.'

'How can I deliver a message to someone I don't even know?'

Judy turned on her friend angrily. 'Oh, for God's sake don't treat me like a child! You know Tam Owen. You've had dealings with him. You've spoken to him on the phone. Not once but hundreds of times.'

The doctor in charge of the case had insisted on putting Linda to bed as soon as she had arrived. There were bandages on her shoulders, which were supported by soft, downy pillows. The whole of one side of her face was obscured by a dressing held in place by a bandage which encircled her head. Only the eye was visible and it was surrounded by a purple, yellowy discoloration. In a basket on a chair within reach of her hand the Siamese cat, Chow, slumbered peacefully.

'Judy, why do you think I'm in here?' Linda said in a low voice. 'Why do you think I'm going to have this bloody operation? Tam Owen did this to me because he thought—'

'Linda,' Judy cut in with exasperation. 'All I'm asking you to do is pass on a message. If I knew Owen, if I knew how to contact him, I'd do it myself.'

Linda stirred cautiously on her pillows, wincing as she felt the dressings shift on the wounds on her shoulders.

'What – what is this message?'

Judy sat down on the edge of the bed. 'Tell him that I've been to see you. Tell him that I've returned to your flat and that I want to talk to him. Ask him to come and see me here tomorrow morning.'

Linda was already shaking her head. 'He won't see you. He'll send Marty Smith and you know what that little bastard—'

'He can't send Marty. The police have picked him up. They're holding him on a murder charge.'

Linda's grin of pleasure was a one-sided affair as half her face was paralysed. But her delight showed in her eyes.

'When did this happen?'

'Linda, I haven't got a lot of time. I've got to be back in town for lunch. Will you do this for me – or won't you?'

'Supposing I do,' Linda said slowly. 'Supposing I do phone Tam Owen and he asks me *why* you want to see him. What, do I say?'

'Tell him I want Peter's job. The same flat, the same terms, the same set-up.'

'You mean you want to work for Owen?' Linda's tone was so scandalised that Chow woke up and peered enquiringly at his mistress. 'You can't be serious!'

'I'm deadly serious,' Judy assured her. 'I'm sick to hell of playing around, Linda. I know the sort of money Peter was making. I also know how he operated. There's no reason why I shouldn't take over, the job he was doing and make it pay just as well.'

'But only the other day you told me you didn't know about Peter. You said you thought he was running some sort of property racket.'

'Look, Linda.' Judy consulted her watch and stood up. 'I've got to have an answer. Will you ring Tam Owen for me? You've got nothing to lose. I think you'll find he'll be very grateful to you.'

'All right,' Linda admitted after a moment. 'I'll ring him. But I think you're making a terrible mistake. If you take my advice—'

Judy rounded on her with an expression which Linda had never seen on her face before.

'I don't want your advice, Linda. I just want you to do what I'm asking.'

'I'll phone tonight. But he won't play. He won't agree to see you.'

'I think he will.'

'You don't know Tam Owen.'

'No, and he doesn't know me.' Judy pressed the lighted end of her cigarette on to the ash-tray and began to twist it viciously. Her voice was as hard as winter grit. 'Tell him I was a friend of Arnold Conway's. A very close friend.'

She straightened up and looked directly into Linda's troubled face.

'Tell him we used to have cosy little chats together.'

*

Judy had never felt so alone in her life. She had arrived at Defoe Mansions an hour earlier. Harry had made her do the last part of the journey on her own. He had a suspicion that Tam Owen or one of his men would be watching the place from now on.

It was little comfort to her that she could look out of the window and see the pedestrians and traffic below, going on with their business as if this was just an ordinary day of the week. Sounds reached her from the neighbouring flats – a dog barking, somebody's baby yelling, the metallic clatter of a dustbin lid.

She could not settle down. Every time she went into the hall the horror of what had happened to Linda in that bedroom swept over her. What was it about Harry Dawson that gave him_ the power to persuade her to try something as risky as this? She wished he could be here in the flat with her, or even that she knew where he was.

Soon after ten-thirty the phone rang, sending an electric shock of fear through her. She answered, but the caller did not speak, simply hung up.

Tam Owen? Checking to see if she was there?

For the tenth time she stood by the window, staring down at the street without moving the curtains. A man in a short rainproof coat with neatly clipped hair was strolling along the opposite pavement. He never glanced at Defoe Mansions. He seemed entirely absorbed by the displays in the shop windows. If she had not encountered Nat Fletcher when he was on duty it would never have occurred to her that he was a police officer.

Not a sign of Harry.

In an effort to make the time pass more quickly she went into the kitchen and made herself a cup of coffee. She was smoking continuously and already four stubs had been crushed out in ashtrays scattered around the flat.

She had the cup to her lips when the doorbell rang. She put it down, noting that her hand had begun to tremble. The kitchen clock gave the time as only ten to eleven.

Had he decided to come early? Would Nat and Harry realise that he had advanced the time by ten minutes?

She hesitated, wondering whether it would be best to ignore any calls before the appointed time. The bell rang again.

She had to know. With beating heart she went to the front door, paused for a moment with her hand on the latch, then opened it.

The man standing on the doormat was a complete stranger, but there was something reassuring about his apologetic, gullible manner. He seemed as surprised as she was.

'Oh!' he exclaimed, then remembered his manners and raised the rather cheeky little felt hat he was wearing. 'Good morning.'

'Good Morning.'

'Can I have a word with Miss Wade, please?'

She studied him curiously. Could this possibly be – No, he must be one of Linda's 'gentlemen friends'. She had a special appeal for these middle-aged, rather bashful men.

'I'm afraid she's not here at the moment.'

'Oh – oh, dear!' He half turned away, eyes cast down. 'How very unfortunate.'

Though you could never be quite sure, it was hardly likely that he'd come at this hour of the morning to avail himself of Linda's services.

She said helpfully: 'Can I help you? I'm a friend of Miss Wade's.'

'Well – my name is Heaton. Sidney Heaton.' As he gave his name he looked at her in a confiding sort of way. 'I have a pet shop in St. John's Wood, and Linda – er, Miss Wade—'

'Oh, yes, of course. I've heard Linda speak of you. Do come in, Mr. Heaton.'

'Er – thank you.'

The contact with another human being, especially such a defenceless creature as Sidney Heaton, was reassuring. Yet with the time moving on towards eleven she could not afford to have him settling down for a long chat. She stopped in the hall and left the door slightly open.

'Linda's away,' she explained. 'She's having an operation. I doubt whether she'll be home until the end of the week.'

'Oh. I didn't realise that. I thought – Well, it's not important.'

He stood awkwardly, holding his hat with both hands, darting frequent glances towards the sitting-room as if he hoped that Linda might, after all, materialise.

'Are you sure I can't help you?'

'No. It's very kind of you but—' She thought that his way of talking in jerky, unfinished sentences must indicate some deep lack of confidence. 'Well – it's just that Miss Wade said she might be interested in buying another Siamese cat and I've seen – She has one already, you know.'

'Yes. I know. Chow.'

Judy had heard the lift begin to ascend. Through the partially open door she saw the number 1 glow as it reached the first floor.

'That's right. Chow,' Heaton went on. 'A sweet little thing. Yesterday a customer of mine brought me another one – just like Chow – an absolute darling. Perfect pedigree. I feel sure she'd sell it if the price was right—'

'Why don't you phone Linda and have a word with her about it? In any case, I'm sure she'd be pleased to hear from you.' The number 2 had illuminated and was now glowing steadily. Whoever was using the lift had got out of the second floor. 'She's in the Maylee Park Nursing Home, St. Albans.'

'Can you give me the number?' Heaton had started to reach for his pocket notebook.'

'I'm afraid not,' she said, moving round to usher him out. 'But it's bound to be in the book.'

'Thank you. That's a very good idea. I'll do that.' He hesitated, still interested in the sitting-room, then pulled the door open. 'It's really very kind of you. Goodbye, Miss – er?'

She shook the offered hand but did not take the hint to give him her name.

She managed to summon up a smile, then closed the door and leaned her back on it. Five to eleven. She took a deep breath and started towards the living-room.

She had not crossed the threshold when the bell sounded again. She halted in her tracks. There had just been time for someone to come up quietly by the staircase from the second floor.

Strangely enough it took an even bigger effort to open the door this second time. When she did so the anti-climax was equally great.

'I'm terribly sorry to trouble you again, but – did you say the nursing home was called Merton?'

He had his notebook and pencil in his hand. Clearly he had decided to write the address down before taking the lift.

'No. Maylee.' She spelt the name out.

'Yes, of course.' Heaton gave an apologetic little laugh. 'How very stupid of me! Now whatever made me think it was Merton?'

Judy repeated the address as if dictating it to a child.

'Yes. I've got it now. I'm not terribly bright this morning, I'm afraid.'

Was it an act? Was he simply carrying out a kind of reconnaissance before deciding to put his cards on the table?

'If you'd like to come in, Mr. Heaton, I'll write it down for you.'

'No, it's all right,' Heaton said after only a moment's hesitation. 'I can remember it now, I'm quite sure.'

He raised his hat again. 'Thank you again. You've been most helpful.'

A draught was blowing through the flat. It caught the door as she was closing it and made it bang more violently than she intended.

Still puzzled, she went towards the sitting-room. She saw immediately that the door leading to the bedroom was wide open. It had been closed when she left the room.

Suddenly she knew that there was someone watching her from behind. She whirled round.

Nat Fletcher was sitting on one of the stools in front of the ornate cocktail cabinet.

He gave her a reassuring nod as he saw her relax.

'How did you get in?' she demanded, furious at the fright he had given her.

'Your favourite fire-escape.' He pointed towards the bedroom. 'You look frightened.'

'I am,' Judy admitted. 'I'm scared to hell.'

'Don't worry. It'll be all right. Everything's under control.'

She searched around for the cigarette she had been smoking when Heaton arrived, could not find it and took one from the rapidly diminishing packet. Nat watched her hands as she fumbled with the lighter. As she drew the first breaths deep into her lungs, a clock somewhere nearby was striking the hour.

'That man who just called,' she said. 'He told me his name was Sidney Heaton. Do you think he—'

'Don't worry.' Nat tapped the miniature radio set tucked into the top pocket of his jacket. 'We've been keeping tabs on him ever since he entered the area—'

He was interrupted by the sudden shrilling of the phone. Judy spun round to stare at it.

'Bang on time.' Nat slid off the stool. 'Now don't forget. Play it cool.'

She moved very slowly to the telephone, her eyes never leaving it. Nat stood very still at a point from which he could see down the hall and into the bedroom.

Judy made a visible effort to summon up her courage, put down her cigarette and picked up the phone.

'Hallo . . . Yes, Mr. Owen. This is Judy Black . . . Why don't you come up?'

Nat nodded approvingly. The tone of voice was good. Now that the action had started her nervousness had gone.

'Why should I want to trap you? It's money I want. In return for evidence, of course. Evidence which could put you in prison for a very long time, Mr. Owen.'

As she listened, she felt the same draught on her back. She turned round and saw Harry coming on tip-toe through the door from the bedroom.

'Don't forget. I knew Arnold Conway too. Knew him a lot better than you realised, I think. Anyway, you remember when you got him to snatch the little dog, Zero? Well, the collar Zero was wearing had some very incriminating information hidden in it. That's why Arnold gave Peter a different collar, which he showed to Mrs. Rogers. But you know all that now, of course, don't you?'

She threw an appealing look at Harry, conveying to him that she could not keep this up much longer. He held up his right hand with the index finger and thumb pressed together. She'd seen him use that gesture before. It meant: 'You're doing fine.'

'You know very well, because Arnold Conway decided to take over Mrs. Rogers' blackmailing enterprises, didn't he? He was trying to take you for £50,000 '

Harry could hear the man's voice crackling in the receiver but he was unable to make out the words. He moved closer to her.

'All right,' Judy continued in that hard tone which she could use so effectively. 'But Arnold was not quite as rash as you thought . . . No, you see he thought you might try something. So, as a precaution, he gave me the evidence to look after.'

Her face was tense as she waited for the reply.

'How much?' She gave a hard little laugh. 'Well, I won't be as greedy as Arnold. Let's just say £20,000 in cash, shall we? Yes, £20,000.'

There was silence for a time, then Harry heard the man make some sort of suggestion. Judy glanced round at him in alarm.

Well Mr. Owen, how can I be sure that I can trust you?'

Harry signalled to her to cover the mouthpiece with her. hand. When she had done so he whispered urgently: 'Tell him you'll give him a sample of the evidence for £1,000, the rest to follow.'

Judy nodded. Her face had gone pale. 'No, Mr. Owen, that's too risky. I'll bring you part of the information. And you bring a thousand pounds. just to show mutual good faith. We can talk about the rest when we meet. All right?'

She listened intently, her fingers repeatedly tapping the ash off the cigarette in her hand.

'Yes . . . yes. I've got that. Cannon Street . . . Goodbye.'

She put the receiver down and leaned against the table. The two men gave her a moment to recover.

'Well?' Nat broke the short silence.

'I'm to take the underground to Charing Cross. He has to draw the money from his bank and it's near there, he says.' 'What do you do when you get there?'

'I'm to stand outside the Embankment entrance and wait until someone contacts me.'

It was the slack hour of the morning and the St. John's Wood underground station was not crowded. Judy had bought an underground ticket more times than she could count, but today she was all thumbs, dropping money on the ground and then trying to go on without her change.

She was on her own again now, though she knew that Nat, Harry and half a dozen other plain-clothes men were not so far away. She dared not look round to see who was following her. Harry had warned her that she might be under observation all the way from Defoe Mansions to Charing Cross. It was essential to behave as if she were going alone to the rendezvous.

Trains were running at longer intervals now, having carried several million passengers to their place of work. A sparse crowd had collected on the platform, spacing themselves out to wait patiently for the train. It was a comfort to feel that so many normal law-abiding people surrounded her. An instinct for self-preservation took her to the place where there were most passengers.

She stared fixedly at the advertisement on the curved wall opposite her. It depicted two girls severed at the waist, only their lower halves visible, discussing the marvellous new jobs they had found. She felt eyes on her back and could not resist the temptation to look round.

A young man was standing behind her, an expression of pleasurable admiration on his face as he contemplated her figure. She turned back quickly, trying not to show the pleasure she always felt when she knew a man was admiring her. To judge by the smile he was neither a detective nor one of Owen's hirelings. He seemed to be the kind of man who would come to her rescue if she appealed to him.

From far away down the black tunnel came the roar of the approaching train. The wind it pushed ahead of itself rushed along the platform and she put up a hand to brush back the strand of hair that had blown on to her, forehead. Then the leading coach burst into the lighted area and the train began to slow. Facing towards it she scanned the passengers on the platform, but could see no sign of Nat or Harry.

The people quickly fanned out with the reaction of experienced travellers, judging exactly at what spot the doors of the carriages would open.

The train was more than half empty, so there was no need to bustle for a seat. She entered by one of the doors at the extreme end of the carriage and sat in a seat close to it. With relief she noted that Nat Fletcher had climbed aboard at the opposite end. He had opened his newspaper and was paying no attention to her at all. A quick inspection of the dozen other people in the carriage reassured her. None of these could be Tam Owen. The young man had chosen a seat on the opposite side a little farther up from which he could admire Judy's legs.

There was the usual sound of hurrying feet as latecomers broke into a run to catch the train. A tallish man in a dark-grey suit with a rolled umbrella dangling from his forearm and a bowler hat on his head stepped unhurriedly into the compartment.

He paused in front of Judy. She looked up to see him smiling down at her. He indicated the empty seat beside her.

'May I, Miss Black?'

She nodded, pursing her lips. This was the moment she had to keep her head. Harry's hunch had been right after all.

He sat down beside her. The doors were still wide open and the train was making its characteristic ticking noise. The driver was waiting for the signalman to give him clearance. It was strange how silent a train full of people could be as it waited in the station. No murmur of conversation, no excited shouts. Just this steady ticking, like a monstrous clock.

She said in a low voice: 'I thought you said I was to wait outside the—'

'A change of plan,' he said affably, and patted his brief-case. 'It's all right. I have the money.' He twisted round to smile at her. 'Not that I expect to need it.'

'Oh? Why not, Mr. Owen?'

'Rogers, please.' Hubert put on his pained look. 'I far prefer my – er – professional name on these occasions. Hubert Rogers.'

The train changed its tune and began to emit the generator-charging hum which indicated preparation to move off. Rogers cocked his ear to it.

'Why won't you need the money?' Judy knew that her voice was shaking. She tried to tell herself that she had nothing to fear.

Hubert was still smiling in his friendly way. 'Because I think you're bluffing me, Miss Black. That's why.'

Judy opened her mouth but she stifled the words as she saw that Hubert's expression had completely changed. And when he spoke his voice had changed too.

'Do you think I haven't met this situation before?' he said quietly. 'Do you think it's new to me?'

'What – situation?' She was almost hypnotised by his voice; she could not even bring herself to even fling a glance towards Nat.

'A girl overhears something – finds something out. Something about me.' He was speaking rapidly, his mouth close to her ear. 'She feels important. It gives her a misguided sense of power. She decides to risk—'

'Mind the doors!'

Hubert had broken off as the familiar chant echoed down the station. The warning was unnecessary. The platform was empty. Those boarding the train were seated and the few who had alighted at St. John's Wood had disappeared up the staircases. Judy risked a glance towards Nat Fletcher.

Suddenly a hand was clamped on her wrist. Hubert had stood up. He moved quickly to the sliding door and got his foot against it to prevent it shutting as all along the train the doors slid across.

'Come on, Judy,' he said brightly. 'This way.'

He propelled her through the door and as he removed his foot and followed her the train began to move.

It accelerated rapidly, so that by the time the end of the carriage passed it was moving quite fast. Judy just had time to see Nat Fletcher, vainly trying to pull the automatic doors apart. He was trapped behind the glass. The train carried him away and into the dark tunnel.

'A friend of yours, Miss Black?' Hubert enquired coldly. 'How many others were there, I wonder?'

He changed his grip, twisting her wrist and forcing her hand up between her shoulder blades. The agonising pain made her scream. He had chosen the arm where the shoulder had been dislocated. As he walked her to the exit the platform was empty and half the train had disappeared into the tunnel.

Harry had been waiting for the train at the extreme end of the platform, where the end of the last carriage had stopped. When he had seen Nat enter the same compartment as Judy he had said a word to the railwayman in charge of the doors and stepped into the little control booth at the back of the train.

All the same, Hubert's manoeuvre had caught him by surprise. When the automatic doors were closed he believed that he had Hubert Rogers nicely sealed up in the same compartment as Nat.

As the train gathered speed he saw to his horror the couple standing on the platform, the girl's arm in the grip of the man's. He pushed past the railwayman, who was standing beside his half-open door.

'Hold it, mate! You want to kill yourself?'

The train must have been travelling at nearer thirty than twenty when Harry jumped out. He had no chance of staying on his feet. He went into a jockey's roll and the very speed of his landing took the jolt out of the impact. He slid along the platform and fetched up against the end wall.

He was bruised and shaken but still conscious. Hubert and Judy had disappeared.

He scrambled to his feet and raced along the platform. In the time available there was only one exit they could have reached. He turned the corner. The staircase ahead was empty. He raced up it, taking the steps three at a time, turned the next corner and there they were near the top of the next flight.

Hubert heard the hurrying footsteps behind him and whirled round. When he saw Harry he thrust his free hand under the lapel of his jacket and drew out a revolver. But he did not aim it at Harry. He thrust the barrel against Judy's chest. The threat of the gesture was unmistakable.

'Keep back, Dawson. Well back. Come up one step and she gets it.'

He began to move away, watching Harry all the time. He must have tightened his grip on the arm, for Judy gasped out loud and her face contorted.

Paradoxically it was that small act of vicious cruelty which brought about Hubert's downfall. The pain made Judy desperate and the sight of her agonised face steeled Harry to risk anything.

As Hubert glanced behind him to see whether all was clear round the next corner, she stamped her sharp heel on that vulnerable part of the human anatomy, his instep. In an instinctive movement of retaliation, he raised the gun to whip her across the face with its hard jaggedness.

Harry saw the momentary opening and flung himself at the man. His momentum threw him between Judy and Hubert. Hubert released his hold on Judy's arm, but as the two men fell to the ground he still had a firm grip on the gun. He was slightly on top of Harry, whose head had struck one of the steps.

Hubert was trying to force the barrel round against Harry when a fury hit him from behind. Judy flung herself on the gun, seizing it with both hands to prevent Hubert aiming it at Harry. Then she dipped her head and sank her teeth into the back of his hand, felt them bite through flesh and blood to the bone beneath.

Hubert howled and relaxed his grip. The gun clattered on to the stone step. She picked it up and stood back, covering him. Hubert took one look at her expression and knew that she was capable in that moment of emptying the chamber into his body. He put his bleeding hand to his mouth, sucking at the wound.

'Don't,' he said. 'Don't shoot.'

He knew what was going through Judy's mind. Not just the pain he had inflicted on her, but Linda Wade's ruined looks, Peter Newton's callous murder, the sacrificial deaths of Tom Dawson and Arnold Conway.

'For God's sake, Dawson,' he said as Harry got to his feet. 'Get that gun from her.'

Harry moved round beside Judy.

'I'll take the gun, Judy. Don't worry. If he gets up off his knees I'll kill him.'

Twenty minutes later Judy and Harry stood on the pavement outside St. John's Wood Station. They were silent as they watched Hubert Rogers, now handcuffed to a uniformed constable, being hustled quickly through the crowd and into the back of a police car. It drew away from the kerb and soon its flashing blue light disappeared among the thickening midday traffic.

The pavement was wet from a recent shower, but now the sun had come out again. Everything seemed very clear and gleaming.

Harry turned to Judy, whose injured arm was tucked under her coat, resting on the button for support.

'Thank you, Judy. Without your help we'd never—' He broke off. It was hard to find the right words. 'What are you going to do now?'

'I feel like a strong cup of coffee,' Judy said. 'Preferably with a tot of whisky in it.'

'That's not a bad idea. But I mean – after that?'

She stared up the street, not really seeing it. The wisp of hair had worked loose again and was playing over her brow.

'I don't know. I've been offered a job in Manchester, but I'm not sure whether to take it or not. I thought I might go away for a week or two. I feel I've earned a holiday.'

'That's a good idea. Why don't you go to The Priory at Steeple Aston? It's quiet, it's a very nice hotel and as I told you, the manager and his wife are friends of mine.'

'Yes. I might do that.' She turned towards him, a slightly mischievous smile playing round her lips. 'Steeple Aston. I suppose that would mean catching a train from Paddington?'

'No,' Harry said with mock seriousness. 'Certainly not Paddington.'

'Euston, then?'

'No.'

'King's Cross?'

Harry shook his head again and they both laughed. He took her firmly by the arm, the good arm, and led her towards a coffee bar a hundred yards down the road.

'You don't take a train at all. Let's go and have that coffee and I'll tell you my plan for solving the problem.'